STAGGERWING

Stories by
Alice Kaltman

STAGGERWING

Stories by Alice Kaltman

Tortoise Books
Chicago, IL

FIRST EDITION, OCTOBER 2016

Staggerwing, Stories © *2016 by Alice Kaltman*

All rights reserved under International and Pan-American Copyright Convention

Published in the United States by Tortoise Books. (www.tortoisebooks.com)

ISBN-10: 0-9860922-7-4
ISBN-13: 978-0-9860922-7-5

Tortoise Books Logo Copyright © 2012 by Tortoise Books. Original artwork by Rachele O'Hare.

For Selma

Contents

Stay A While 1

Freedom 23

Boss Man 31

Snow Day! 59

A Melody 87

Blossoms 111

Stranger in Paradise 131

Staggerwing 159

Bigfoot 183

The Honeymoon Suite 207

Tossed 221

Stay A While

I needed a goddamn purpose. Everyone around me was, pardon the lingo, finding themselves. Women my age were going on yoga retreats, throwing clay, volunteering at homeless shelters. None of that appealed to me, and I wasn't going to do something just for the sake of doing something. It stuck in my craw that there I was, 70 years old, without a clue as to what to do. I'd spent years trudging along, raising kids, feeding a family, being an undemanding faculty wife. It hadn't been some soap opera, not like some people's I knew. Quite the opposite. It had been pretty darn boring.

At least the other old gals ended up with flexible spines, leaky flower vases, or goody-good self satisfaction. All I had was my craw and the yucky feeling stuck in it.

+++++++

Things started to change on one of those brain-numbing but bright winter days, the kind of day God created to make me feel like a lazy, resistant fool because the last thing I wanted to do was step outside and freeze my patootey off. I was taking a break from folding laundry, kerplopped on the cellar stairs, slurping some tepid Lipton's and surveying the crappy reality of my 'finished basement.'

The ping-pong table covered with file boxes filled with ancient tax returns: shreddable, decades old.

My husband Kevin's saggy punching bag, hanging useless in the corner like a bum at an abandoned bus stop.

My son Greg's teddy bear slumped in a beanbag chair. What was that bear's name again? Grayface. That was it. Such an unoriginal name. But Greg had never been the most creative child, so no surprises there.

My daughter Sophie's pink Barbie roller skates. Did anyone even roller skate anymore? Sophie surely didn't. Now it was yoga. Yoga, yoga, yoga. Or triathlon training. All she ever talked about on the rare occasions I actually saw her in the flesh.

The deflated hoppity hop ball. The outdated VCR. The badminton birdies. All those spiky little Legos. Piles of skirts and slacks from a different era, a long-ago size.

And the wet bar. Kevin's idea, of course. A nine-foot-long red-leather studded embarrassment. For entertaining, or so he'd said back when we'd installed it forty years earlier. We'd had guests down there five times, tops, and all those boozy parties were within the first year. I wasn't much for entertaining. And back then if the wife didn't make the social plans, then there were no social plans. Mostly Kevin used the bar to sneak shots while I was upstairs attending to two toddlers, a task I found brutally boring. Motherhood hadn't been a sparkly fiesta for me. I myself was an only child, raised on a farm by uninspired parents. Hand me a slippery, grimy hog, no problem. But wiggly and whiny children? No siree, Bob.

I got up from my seat slowly, the knees a touch arthritic. It was time to get back upstairs to the good old daily grind. I took one last look around the basement and thought: what a waste of space.

Later that evening I was watching HGTV on the old portable black-and-white while fixing Kevin's dinner. That home renovation show with those handsome young twins was on. You know the show I mean. The real estate agent twin is a snappy dresser and the other one has a bit more facial hair. Anyway, that's when it came to me. A sputtering lightbulb of an idea. What if I fixed the cellar up, rented it out? I was a hard worker. Renovating the basement could be my purpose. Heck. There was money to be made.

I couldn't care less if Kevin put up a fuss. Since he'd retired from the Comp Lit department he did all his drinking upstairs anyway. No more trips to the basement to sneak a few. Sometimes he walked over to the Faculty Club where he found a captive audience for his long-winded monologues. I'll bet his former colleagues nodded their heads, pretending to listen, thanked their lucky stars that Kevin had finally retired. Lord knew he'd made a hash of it as Chair.

+++++++

"The basement has always been creepy," I said over ham loaf and green beans. "Even after we loaded it with toys, the kids never really liked playing down there."

"Ah ha," Kevin twirled his fork in the air. Here it comes I thought, some edict from on high. "That's because their impressionable minds were filled with horrific images from all that TV you let them watch. Monsters lurking behind basement doors. If you'd encouraged them to read every now and then..."

Neither of our kids was big into books. But who could blame them, with Kevin breathing down their necks, spewing sermons about literary crap for hours every night? As soon as they left home, they went as far afield from academia as possible. Sophie, an anorexic exercise junkie and Greg, an unambitious Dunkin' Doughnuts franchise owner.

"People make a killing on these short-term home rentals. We can rent it to visiting professors. Or parents. Or those alumni who take over the town on Homecoming Weekend."

Kevin shook his head. "The idea of total strangers in my basement causes me a great deal of unease." With another loose wave of his Scotch-holding hand he added, "Who knows what evil lurks in the heart of men? The Shadow knows."

"We can use the extra money." I said. Kevin sliced his ham loaf. His knife hand was relatively steady, but his head was wobbling like a dashboard doggie's. Four drinks already. Three sheets to the wind. "Your pension is peanuts."

He looked at me with nothing good in his stare. He was glowering. Glowering. How's that for a good literary word from a good literary wife? Then he mumbled something sloshy.

"I can gussy the place up for next to nothing."

"Ha. Next to nothing. I've heard that before," Kevin grumbled.

"Get a grip," I snapped. "I'm no spendthrift and you know it."

Kevin heaved one of his dramatic, condescending sighs. "Suit yourself, Martha Stewart."

I got up and took my plate to the garbage and dumped the remains deep in the bin's belly. My plate made a clackety-clack racket as I tossed it in the sink.

+++++++

The next morning, I pulled out the Yellow Pages and let my fingers do the walking. I hired Pedro and Carlos, an Ecuadorian handyman duo, to help me transform the basement. They rewired the whole kit and caboodle, turned the wet bar into a kitchenette, scraped and repainted the walls, laid a decent sisal carpet over the cold cement floor, installed new fixtures, and added a shower stall in the mildewed half bath last used in the early nineties by Greg and his pot-smoking friends.

I didn't bother to call the kids to see if they wanted any of their old stuff. Why open up that can of worms? I'd held on long enough. I dropped garbage bags heaped with clothes and toys at Goodwill. The old files were shredded at the local Staples. The VCR player went curbside and was gone the next morning along with the bean bag chair.

I forgot to return phone calls. Library books went overdue. Milk soured. Midwestern dust settled on every possible household surface. Kevin was left to fend for himself for many meals, which he really didn't mind because it was another excuse to head down to the Club, blab away, get soused, and eat overrated hamburgers, courtesy of the university.

I felt great, as if I were a Broadway producer putting on a show. I shopped for furnishings and decor and kept my purchases as far from Kevin as possible. I avoided him like the plague. Not that we spent much time together anymore in the first place. But while I was on such a roll, the last thing I needed were more snarky Martha Stewart comments.

+++++++

Six weeks later the apartment was good as gold, and I was ready to start my new purposeful career. The night before the first guests were due, I thought: why not inaugurate the place? Do a test run? At 9 pm I shuffled past the TV room door in bathrobe and slippers, a shower caddy swinging in my hand, a towel draped jauntily over my shoulder. I felt giddy, like I was on my way to a fancy spa.

"Well, pray tell. Where the hell are you headed?" Kevin called from his La-Z-Boy throne.

I was feeling so good that I paused and considered asking Kevin to join me. Back in the beginning we'd gone at it like a couple of feral cats. All spray and sweat and sauciness. He claimed to get hard just thinking about my country girl naiveté. I'd get wet if he as much as uttered one line of his fancy-pants poetry.

Now I glanced at Kevin as he glanced at the TV. The scotch glass rested on his bloated belly, moving up and down with each wheezy breath. Pale flesh and grey hairs poked out between the straining buttons of his Oxford shirt. The shirt I'd ironed that afternoon that now looked like a wrinkled rag. I waited for a smidgen of the old randiness to bubble up in me. But nope. Nothing there. That ship had sailed a long time ago.

"I'm going to check out the accommodations," I said.

"Ah oui. Le grand appartement," Kevin drawled. "Don't forget to change the boudoir sheets après."

Mr. Maurice Chevalier. As if I would've forgotten. "I wasn't born in a barn, Kevin," I sighed. "Even if I was raised on a farm."

He lifted his glass. "Touché." He glugged the diluted dregs. He'd be back at the liquor cabinet in moments, but for now he fiddled with the remote and turned the volume way up. Birds screeched. A nature

[7]

show. The sound of crows chased me down the basement stairs.

Peace finally came once I lay down on the brand new apartment bed. After a few minutes paging through a National Geographic plucked from the magazines I'd arranged fan-styled on the nightstand, I was ready for sleep. I snapped off the reading lamp and settled in like a chicken cutlet sandwiched between crispy 400-count cotton sheets. I tossed my arms overhead, letting my fingers trace the carvings of the brand new pine headboard. I shut my eyes and breathed deeply, enjoying the smell of fresh paint and carpet glue. New starts should always smell slightly toxic, I thought as I drifted off.

+++++++

I wish I could tell you that from then on I was a happy, purposeful woman. But things weren't that simple. Sooner than you can say jackrabbit, renting the apartment became all-consuming in very tedious ways. The bookings. The Paypal account. The chit-chat and small talk with prospective customers. The online ordering of replacement towels and pillow cases. The tidying, the vacuuming, the shower scrubbing. The mystery stain removals. There I was, doing what I'd done my whole adult life: cleaning up after people. A tired old workhorse. It didn't feel purposeful. It felt like slave labor.

+++++++

[8]

After about three months of rental monotony, I found a scarf while stripping the bed. I'd seen Adrianne Wiener with this scarf fluffed under her chin the day she and her husband checked in to the apartment for their four-day, three-night stay. It was one of those wispy, barely-there scarves that women of a certain age knot around their necks to obscure their droopy skin. There it was, wedged between the headboard and mattress, like a secret. Like a sign.

I sat down on the bed and fingered the silk. I'd never been a scarf wearer myself, too fussy for my tastes, though I do have quite the turkey wattle that could use a cover up. So I don't know what compelled me to do what I did next. I tied the scarf around my own neck, which aside from not being my style, is not something I should've done, because heaven knows what other possibly unsanitary purposes Adrianne Wiener might've used that scarf for, aside from tying it around her age-spotted, wrinkly neck. But there I was, against my better judgement, looping and fluffing it under my very own chin.

Suddenly I felt an odd tingling up my spine, and before I knew it, I was basking in a glow of giddy good humor I'd never felt before. I felt no desire to get up and go, to do my job, to soldier on. I felt like the kind of person who settles in, who knows how to relax. Someone with a chipper attitude. The kind of person who laughs a lot. A passive, happy person. A lighthearted, fun-loving, where's-the-party type of person.

The person I imagined Adrianne Wiener to be.

Mind you, I was not one given to flights of fancy. Cockamamie fantasies were Kevin's domain, with his stacks of unfinished stories, novels, and sonnets accumulating for decades. Him with his Ivy League degrees. Me, barely making it through rural high school. I had enough sense to know what was happening to me didn't have to do with imagination. It was a visitation. I felt right as rain.

Then the honky dory Adrianne Wiener sensations fizzled out, like helium sputtering from a pin-holed balloon. I was back to dull normal after twenty minutes. The used bed linens were in a crumpled heap to my right. The fresh ones to my left. There was still dusting, vacuuming, and scrubbing to do. I needed to get on the horn and confirm a two week booking with some chemistry big shot from Paraguay. So I took Adrianne Wiener's scarf off, shoved it in my apron pocket, and got back to work.

Later that day, the scarf was in a padded envelope laying on the Post Office scale about to be mailed to Adrianne Wiener COD. Just as I was about to close my side of the bullet-proof window and send it on its merry way, I grabbed it back and left the Post Office.

I ripped open the Jiffy Pak in the car, tore up the note I'd put in for Adrienne Wiener, shook out the scarf and tied it around my neck once more. My heart was beating tom-tom fast as I drove home. I wore the scarf for the rest of the day. While I pushed my cart around the supermarket. While I paid bills. I wore it while cooking Kevin's pot roast. I wore it until I undressed and got ready for bed.

I'd like to say it kept me in that easy breezy state of mind, the Adrianne Wiener state of mind, but it didn't. I suppose I felt a bit less me-like, but that might've just been because I was taking a 'fashion risk' wearing the damn scarf at all. I didn't feel transported the same way I had that morning.

But I kept it anyway.

+++++++

I started keeping other forgotten things also. You'd be surprised how often folks leave stuff behind. It's shocking, really. Books, magazines, underwear, toothbrushes, medications, hats, gloves, tiny figurines, photographs, socks. Lots of socks.

I'd test out every lost item. And like a magic spell, each time I'd feel a distinct emotion that was not my own. Far from my own.

Some were horrible. Gut-wrenching despair. Bowel-clearing fear. Panic to beat the band. Visiting professor Charles Huang's copy of Time magazine left me weepy and snot-nosed. The watch cap left by an attractive young man named Colin McGarry caused me such heartache I thought I might die.

[11]

On the other hand, Beth Fartung's sweaty jog bra shot me through with energy and pep, in spite of its rancid stench. The world was my oyster for the twenty minutes I fondled Max Jacob's Polident tube. And my goodness, what Sally Marks' toothbrush did for me!

Yes, I put on other people's undergarments. Stuck their dental hygiene items in my mouth. But please, don't be disgusted. I couldn't help myself. Worlds of emotion had opened to me for the first time in my life. I loved it all. The I-wanna-die moments as tasty as the ain't-life-grand peaks. I was addicted to other folks' feelings.

+++++++

But here's the problem—the problem, that is, aside from sneaking around, sniffing, rubbing, holding, and wearing stuff that didn't belong to me. Each item was only good for one high. After twenty minutes of feeling someone else's feeling, my life resumed its blank and boring regularity.

So I cleaned, I booked, I cleaned again. After each renter left I scoured the apartment hoping they'd been careless. That they'd done me the favor of leaving something marvy behind to kept me afloat. I should have returned the items after I'd gotten high on them, but I'm ashamed to say I didn't. I kept all the Forgottens, as I liked to call them, in a black lawn and leaf bag shoved deep in the rear of my closet. I couldn't part with them.

My own upstairs home was in shambles. No food in the fridge, dust bunnies living in every corner. I would press my ear against the basement door listening for snippets of conversations. I wanted to get an inkling of what goodies I might inhale or rub up against once my renters were gone. Quarrels, giggles, sobs. You name it, I'd take it. I'd stand for hours by my living room window, peeking through my lace curtains at the walkway that led to the outside cellar stairs, hoping to catch a glimpse as these strangers came and went. I wanted to see how they looked when they thought no one was watching. Did they smile? Scowl? Did they trudge, downward and dogged? Was that a skip? A devil-may-care jaunt?

Then, as is the way with addiction, mine got worse. I stopped waiting for turnover time. When the coast was clear—say, when anxious parents left to meet their sophomore son at his dorm, or a nostalgic alum marched off to the Big Game, or that lonely professor went to grab a bite at Chili's—I'd sneak downstairs and swipe stuff. You know, just in case nothing was left behind. A sock here, a hair comb there. Just to keep the mojo going. Nothing anyone would truly miss.

Or so I told myself.

+++++++

Months went by. No one ever suspected me of taking anything. I mean really, look at who I was: An old lady living in a large colonial house on a tree-lined street with my retired academic lush of a husband. What would someone like me want with someone's stinky drawers or crumbled bus ticket?

Almost a year passed when my daughter Sophie deigned to honor us with one of her rare visits. She'd stopped by with our grandkids en route to a local birthday party. Our house was on the way, you see. No bending over backwards for Sophie, unless she was literally bending over backwards in one of her sweaty yoga classes. This was a visit based on convenience. Convenience combined with free booze.

Sophie and I sat in the living room, she with wine and me with my Lipton's while the grandkids wandered around the house looking for trouble.

"Geez Ma. When was the last time you cleaned this place?" Sophie swiped her finger along the dusty glass topped coffee table.

"My back's been bothering me," I lied. "Doctor said to lay off any house work for a couple of weeks. And Lord knows your father isn't going to grab a sponge."

"Well it's not like you ever asked him to," she sighed and took a sip.

Oh, that old tune again, I thought. If I wasn't careful I'd be in for one of her feminist mumbo-jumbo rants.

We were sitting in cranky silence when Kylie, the eight year old, came prancing out of my bedroom holding a pair of black rabbit fur earmuffs.

"Can I have these, Gramma?" she whined.

Kylie had obviously been rummaging in my closet. Gotten her little paws deep into my lawn and leaf bag filled with Forgottens. The earmuffs belonged to Mrs. Smith, a recent two-day, one-night guest. A woman drowning in fountains of worry, but with a kind heart shining through her muck. I knew this because Mrs. Smith's earmuffs had given me twenty minutes of jitters and warm glow. Two feelings for the price of one. A rare double whammy.

"Kylie," Sophie barked. "Don't go grabbing things that don't belong to you."

Kylie ignored her mother and stared at me. "So can I?" She snapped the earmuffs on her head and stood in front of me with a 'come on, do something, you dull old wooden stump' smirk on her face.

I did nothing. I was in a state of shock. I probably did look like a dull old wooden stump, but inside I was watching and waiting. Would the earmuffs work on Kylie? Juice her up? Would she become nervous and kindly? An eight-year-old version of sweet old Mrs. Smith?

Finally I spoke. "How are you feeling, Kylie?"

"Fine," she pouted. "So, can I have 'em?"

Greedy little creature, I thought. Same as always. I kept watching. A change could still be coming.

"Any tingles?" I asked.

A crease as deep as the Missouri River formed between her freckled little brows. "That's a stupid question." Rude as ever.

"Do you feel loving? A little jittery?"

Sophie groaned from her slouched seat on the sofa. "What's with the freaky questions, Ma?"

"Can't I have a conversation with my granddaughter who I never see?" Covering up with a guilt-inducing jab was not my usual style. But desperate times, as the saying goes.

"Gimme a break." Sophie rolled her eyes and took another swig of Chardonnay.

"Puleeeeease, Gramma?" Kylie whined.

I studied my granddaughter. Was that a softening around her eyes? Tension in that pouty little mouth?

Kylie broke the spell. "What. Ever." She turned away from me and skipped towards the den where her little brother Joshy was watching educational cartoons with Kevin.

"I've got a new pair of earmuffs...I've got a new pair of earmuffs..." she sang. From the back she looked like a pint-sized airport worker, wearing giant ear protectors, taxiing planes to the gate.

"Where did you get those earmuffs anyway?" Sophie asked as she chugged her third glass of wine. She drank like a fish. In this, she was her father's daughter. I wondered if her sweaty workouts counteracted the effects.

"On sale at Target," I lied.

"Seriously?" she chuckled. "They're so not you."

But they were, I thought. For twenty blissful minutes a few weeks back, they were very much me.

+++++++

I thought that would be the end of it, but I couldn't stop. Couldn't keep my paws off other people's personalities. I'd slid down a slippery slope.

At least I started nabbing things no one would notice. Used dental floss. Tissues from the garbage pail. Toenail clippings. Not stealing exactly. Discarded trash, really. I was lucky if I got a five-minute high off any of it.

I was at it for another two months, rifling through debris and plucking hairs off pillow cases to support my habit, when the inevitable happened. Sidney Krackowski was three days in to his six-day stay. He'd gone for his morning run. I'd timed him his first two mornings. I had a good forty minutes to go downstairs and find something to nuzzle, sniff, maybe even eat before he returned.

Sidney left me an offer I couldn't refuse. Right smack dab on the nightstand. A Red Sox cap, resting upside down like a candy bowl. It even had a few of Sidney's black curls stuck on the inside brim. I should've just plucked the hairs and sniffed, but there was a greater temptation. I knew what goodies the cap held. I'd eavesdropped Sidney's nightly sob-fest. I'd heard him on his phone begging someone, his wife most likely, to 'please, please reconsider for the kids' sake,' telling her 'I'm lost without you'. I'd noticed his red-rimmed eyes before he snapped on his fancy sunglasses to go jog away the pain every morning.

[17]

Yes, you got it. I put the cap on and lay down on the bed and closed my eyes. Within moments, the tingle started. Soon yummy tears rolled down my cheeks. I was swimming in sadness, a perfect lump in my heart the size of a grapefruit.

Then I heard it. A gasp.

"Mrs. McIntire?"

I opened my eyes. Sidney Krackowski loomed over me, sweat dripping off his forehead and onto my bosom.

I bolted upright and put the cap back on the nightstand. Sidney's sadness left me, replaced with my very own sense of shame. "Ah, well," I stammered. "Is that yours?"

He just stared at me, cockeyed.

I got up off the bed and smoothed my skirt. "Well, geez Louise. Apologies. What a coinky dink. My husband has one just like it. He thought maybe he'd left it down here, before, before..."

Before what?

Sidney picked up his cap, pinching the brim with his thumb and forefinger. He examined it as it dangled from his hand, like a dirty object. Like he might catch something nasty from me.

+++++++

I had to stop. I just had to. No more renting the apartment. Two weeks passed, and all I did was clean the house. Upstairs, that is. Downstairs was no go. Off limits. I knew if I went down there I'd instantly claw the carpet,

[18]

lick the walls, or rub my face on the shower curtain in search of a stray emotion. Instead I wandered from room to room, like a cleaning zombie.

When Kevin asked why I decided to close up shop, I said I'd caught one of the renters sneaking around our home.

"Going through your pile of papers, no less," I lied.

"Aha! You see?" he said. "I told you strangers lurking in our basement was a bad idea." He sat at the dining table with a giant cheese platter in front of him. A 'snack'. He'd been shoveling wedges of cheddar the size of roof shingles into his mouth.

I nodded and sprayed some Lemon Pledge close to his platter.

He kept eating.

I just kept on cleaning.

+++++++

That night, we met our son and his family at Rossetti's Ristorante to celebrate our grandson Brandon's fifth birthday.

I was in a daze for most of the meal. I barely paid attention to the chatter, Kevin's sloshy rants, Greg's boring doughnut stories, my daughter-in-law Karen's attempts to suck me in to womanly drivel, the grandkids knock-knock jokes. Muzak, all of it.

In other words, things were back to normal.

Meanwhile, a tackily-dressed woman was laughing like a hyena at the table next to ours. Her husband was staring down at his plate with a face as red as the marinara sauce dripping over his pasta. I couldn't help but stare, and envy.

I wanted to be in the throes of her yuck-fest, to get as loud and sloppy as she was. Have my own laugh riot. I wanted it so badly I could taste it. When the woman got up from her seat to go to the bathroom, it took every ounce of strength I had not to swipe the tacky beaded shawl off the back of her chair, wrap it around my own shoulders, and wait for the fun to begin.

But instead I turned towards my own family and tried to listen.

"Hey Mom," said Greg, his mouth full of eggplant parmigiana, "Dad tells me you've decided to stop renting the basement apartment."

"Yup," I nodded.

"Well, maybe I should move in for a while," he elbowed his wife. "Get a little rest from the old ball and chain."

Karen elbowed him back. "You're so funny I forgot to laugh."

And then it occurred to me. I looked at them all. My flesh and blood. They were vessels. They had feelings. Okay, maybe not the most pizzazz-y feelings, but feelings all the same. Maybe I could emote off them instead of strangers. The way a conscientious vampire feeds off rodents instead of humans. Keep it all in the family, so to speak. Maybe at least feel...something.

I didn't want to experiment with any of Kevin's shady emotions, and Greg and Karen were too far across the table to steal from. So, while he was busy gleefully bopping his baby brother on the head with a buttered roll, I pulled the straw out of Brandon's chocolate milk and put it in my mouth.

It took a moment before anyone noticed.

Kevin's scotch glass clinked to the table top. "Jesus, woman," he hissed. "What are you doing?"

"I'm waiting," I said.

"Waiting for what?" someone else asked. I don't recall who. I was deep in expectation. Willing that tell-tale tingle to start up my spine. To take me away.

Eventually there was laughter.

But it came from everyone but me. It should've hit me by then.

At least the birthday boy got a good birthday chuckle seeing his old grandma with a striped straw sticking out of her puckered mouth.

But me? I got nothing. I was, and will forever be, the same old, same old me.

Freedom

Oh the burn. That searing pain squeezing his thighs like a vise grip. The supreme feeling. The most validating. Even more affirming than the heaving sensation in his gut. A smaller gut these days. But still a paunch, folded over burning thighs as Danny pedaled fast and furious through the Vermont country side.

Danny had never been a big one for physical pain. But the past few months had changed that. Now he was a glutton for punishment, as long as it came via two wheels, multiple gears and a padded seat. Biking had become his thing. It might smack of mid-life crisis, but no question, it was a healthy outlet. Much better than a trophy wife or sporty car. Not that either of those were viable options for an overweight New York City public school English teacher recently dumped by his high-power executive wife.

The super steep Vermont inclines provided pure bliss. Now another magnificent hill was coming his way. Danny shifted expertly to proper gear. Like the little engine that could, he made his way to the top. I think I can, I think I can...

+++++++

Four months earlier, on a tepidly overcast April afternoon, Danny trudged like a tired refugee towards the subway. Meg had planted the bomb two weeks earlier. Her actual words: It's not working Danny. Our fighting is bad for Cody. You know it and I know it. I want a divorce. The subtext: I'm having the best sex of my life with Craig Gundersen. I'm not that interested in the whole parenting thing. I'm out of here, you fat fuck.

No question who Cody should end up with as far as Danny was concerned. What the courts decided was another matter.

Before descending the subway stairs, he lifted his eyes momentarily, hoping for a glimmer of sunlight, a ray of something akin to hope. It was then Danny spotted the bike, propped in the window of Urban Cyclist, front wheel slightly elevated, as if to create the illusion of flight. The Kestrel Talon. Maybe it was the name, the implication of speed and slice. Or maybe it was how the weak sunlight reflected off the bicycle's silver metal while it barely warmed Danny's disappointed soul. The Kestrel Talon gleamed. It downright beckoned. Danny hadn't ridden a bike in fifteen years. The damn thing set him back two thousand bucks.

He trained every day. Got up at five a.m., headed to Central Park and did the loop, not just once, not just twice. By mid-May it was often ten times. Danny added extra workouts in the afternoons, snuck out of MS 115 like a cat burglar, skipped the useless faculty meetings, let his perpetually delinquent students off without detention. Why waste his breath?

All rides were cathartic. His earliest ones pointedly so. Danny's cycling was feriocious, if uncouth and energy inefficient. His pre-divorce imagination went vividly wild. Danny rounded the 110th Street hill and left a long tar-and-pebbled gash across the sloping asphalt which he fantasized was Meg's formidible ass. The downhill at 72nd Street provided opportunity to hyper-speed along the delicate bridge of Meg's lovely nose. Danny broke it, deviated her septum. Snap, snap, snap. Ah, but the sweetest musing of all came at the southeast corner of 59th, where Danny pumped his brakes to gouge a repeated pattern along the meat of Craig Gundersen's overrated cock.

+++++++

Now it was August, with only a few niggling details of shared custody to work out. Danny had arrived at this remote corner of Vermont two days earlier with the Kestrel Talon secured to the roof of his Prius. He checked in to Olaf's Country Inn, an old farmhouse with a few musty spare rooms near the back entrance. Tomorrow uber-parenting would begin again. Danny would be sitting in the outdoor Arpeggio Lake Music Camp Amphitheatre, trying to covertly swat voracious mosquitoes while his brilliant flute prodigy of a son trilled his way through Mozart. Last year Danny and Meg had come together, sitting closer to each other than they had in years. All for Cody's benefit. Meg would've rather died. She complained about the heat, the uncomfortable, backless outdoor seating, the bugs, the humidity, the other parents. But it was Danny she most abhorred. Danny with his hairy, clammy thigh pressing against her wall of impenetrable smoothness.

But this summer, Danny was in biking heaven. Meg was out at Gundersen's East Hampton compound doing God knew what. Danny couldn't care less. He was in stellar cycling form. There was no more need for revenge riding now that he was such a cycling beast. No decline or coasting or resting before he got to the tippy top of this hill. Just. Going. For. The. Burn.

Hill, meet Danny. Danny, meet Hill.

He crested the top and gave himself a silent cheer. No pause, just an easy coast down, taking in the sights. Danny passed beauty, he passed despair. To his left, gold flowers sprouted through the broken window of a derelict home. Vines with deep purple blossoms twisted around yellow hazard tape on a rusted, wire fence. To his right, a gorgeous green field was filled with abandoned car chassis. If Danny still wrote poetry, this contradictory Vermont landscape would provide inspiration. Better than teaching slow-witted eighth graders to churn out their own half-baked verse, that was for sure.

Danny hit a straightaway. Time to pour on the juice. He looked at the speedometer. 40 mph. Not too shabby. He couldn't help wonder if Craig Gunderson was capable of such a feat. But why think of such things? Danny refocused. Speed was his priority.

There was a minor obstacle just ahead, before another magnificent hill. A dog straining on a chain connected to a stake at the end of the straightaway. Imprisoned on a dusty patch of earth at the foot of a beautiful incline. Another countryside paradox. It looked like a mutt. But what did Danny know about dogs? He'd never owned one. His childhood had been petless. His Depression-era parents had had no extra cash floating around their Flatbush apartment to feed a mouth that wasn't even human. Cody, of course, had always wanted a dog. But Meg was allergic, which was lucky, because Danny was a wee bit scared of dogs.

But Vermont dogs were tolerable, in large part because they were always behind fences, roped to mailboxes, leashed to barns. Or chained to posts like this one. They were shackled, while Danny was free.

The dog edged its front paws on to the asphalt. Toenails click-clacked like castenets as it lurched and howled. It was female, emaciated, but with a bunch of droopy teats.

Danny grunted as he did a clean little loopy loo around the poor, hapless beast. He moved onward and upward. The hill was mighty steep. Danny's breath was shallow. His gut lurched. His heart pumped. And joy of joys, his thighs were killing him! Perfection, but for the continued, desperate yapping of that dog down the hill.

[27]

At the summit, Danny stopped to take a swig of Powerade. He took big gulps of the fresh Vermont air and told himself he was glad to be alive. He gazed behind himself, proud to survey where he'd come from. The dog stared up at him, quiet now. She knew her limits.

"Top o' the mornin' to ya, Ma'am," he called to her with a jaunty and terrible faux-Irish accent.

The dog barked once. Then, with canine decisiveness, she bounded up the hill at quite a clip, the chain and upended stake clanging behind her like tin cans attached to a newlywed's bumper.

Danny scrambled to reattach his cleats, his entire body quaking. He adjusted his gears and after a wobbly start, he careened down the next decline. His breath was shallow. His gut lurched. His heart pumped. But this was panic, not joy.

The dog raced closer, dragging that damn stake and chain. She was fast, for a scrawny little thing.

Danny willed himself to focus on the road ahead. The dog was gaining on him, galloping like a horse. She was so near, Danny could hear her wheezing breath. There was a gurgle and a catch to it. The dog was determined. Maybe desperate too.

The pothole was an unforeseen conclusion. While Danny flew over his handle bars he thought, who will cut the crusts off Cody's peanut butter and banana sandwiches?

He landed with a dull thud. Bruised and scraped, but nothing severed. His extra poundage had cushioned the blow. Before he could get up, the dog was upon him, her paws pressed against his chest. She licked his cheeks, his lips. She slobbered all over his bike goggles, his helmet, his neck.

Her collar was so tight her dun colored fur puffed and swelled around it. Yellow crud coated her lower lids. Her breath was swampy and hot. The dangling teats were dried up, crusted over, spent.

Danny lay still, and let the dog kiss him. There was no need for any more fear. Eventually he reached up to unbuckle her collar. Underneath, the bare doggy skin was red and raw. She paused for a moment, registering this new sensation, breeze on flesh. She sniffed the air, considered the empty road ahead. Then she returned her gaze to Danny with eyes dark as tar, and started kissing him again.

Danny rolled out from under her. Instantly she leaned in to him, her ribs pressing against his sopping wet tunic. Olaf's Inn was less than a quarter mile away. An easy ride. An easy run. There were no other guests. And there was that back entrance after all.

Cody had always wanted a dog.

"Do you know how to keep quiet?" Danny asked.

The dog looked up at him and blinked.

Boss Man

There are no olives in the pantry, and I distinctly remember buying some organic pimento-stuffed ones at Whole Foods yesterday.

Or maybe it was last week.

The point is I need them now for the dish I'm serving tonight at our small, casual dinner party.

Casual. Who am I kidding? There's nothing casual about it.

My husband's new boss Chet is coming with his 'lady friend.' I've never met Chet, but from the way Dimitri describes him, he sounds like a misogynistic, entitled fuckhead. A gazillionaire who never went to college, likes to surround himself with brilliant, young, exploitable employees he treats the way a cat treats a litter box. He actually calls them all 'kiddies,' except for Dimitri, who's the new legal counsel at BangleBrains, and only other person in Chet's 50-something age bracket.

"Dimitri," I yell, "Did you eat my olives?" My husband has a tendency to raid the kitchen for anything savory. A deep love of salt runs in his Greek family, and Dimitri uses his ethnicity as an excuse for these briny binges.

"No," he says. I startle and turn to find him sitting behind me at the kitchen table, clipping his fingernails, gently coaxing each crescent into a neat little pile.

"That is so completely disgusting," I say calmly. "We eat at that table. Our children eat at that table."

"Our children don't live here anymore Amanda." He keeps clipping. "We're empty nesters, remember? Hurrah!"

Our youngest, Adam left two weeks ago to start his freshman year studying 'Theater Arts' at a respectable Midwestern institution; he was immediately surrounded by a sea of suspiciously friendly students from all those 'I' states; Illinois, Indiana, Iowa. He called last Saturday and said, "Everything is super." Super? Where is my sardonic, little Brooklyn boy?

Whatever the case, I've never liked nest analogies, empty or otherwise. Avian imagery indicates flightiness. Plus, more than ever these days, what I need is serious grounding. Sandbags-tied-to-my-ankles grounding. And it's not just because the kids are gone.

"Big Whoop, Dimitri," I make a little circle in the air with my index finger. "Meanwhile, I can't find the olives I bought at Whole Foods...whenever. I need them for my pasta dish."

"You're making your pasta dish?" He's working on his left pinky, trying for a single clip.

"Is there a problem with that?"

Dimitri shrugs.

"I thought you loved my pasta dish. The feta cheese, the anchovies, the basil, the olives..."

"I do love it," he hesitates, "It's just that I thought you'd make something more, um, unusual tonight."

"What? I'm supposed to go catch a pig and roast it on a spit for your new boss?"

"No..."

"Maybe the pig could go sniff out some truffles in the backyard before I burn his grunty rump?"

"Amanda..."

I collapse in to the seat across from him. There's a stray nail clipping on my side of the table. I grasp it between two fingers, drop it in his pile, then lay my forehead on the cool glass table top. "I hate dinner parties," I moan.

"No you don't. You just hate Chet. Hypothetically."

I look up and give Dimitri my forlorn, Bambi-has-lost-his-mother look.

"Maybe he'll surprise you. Maybe you'll like him," Dimitri always looks for the sunny side of things. "Some women find him quite charming." He scoops his clippings off the edge of the table in to his waiting palm, examining his collection with pride.

"Chet's 'lady friend' for instance," I say, returning my forehead to the glass. "I'll bet she's a piece of work."

Dimitri doesn't respond. I look up, and realize he's left the room.

[33]

+++++++

Dimitri got me another jar of olives. He also bought me a bunch of roses. Yellow roses, which are my favorite.

"Your pasta will be a smash hit," he says. "I'm an idiot. I don't know how you put up with me."

I kiss him and refrain from commenting on his bad olive-y breath. Because, really, in the husband department it doesn't get any better than Dimitri. Even if he tends towards the unshaven, stinky side. Even if he's got weird eating habits. He puts up with my critical know-it-all tendencies. He's a great dad to our two sons, the aforementioned Adam, and our eldest, Emmett, who's doing his medical residency up in Boston. (A provincial, parochial excuse for a city, if you ask me.)

And boy, oh boy, did Dimitri step up to the plate when the debacle began.

He took better care of me than Snow White took of all the dwarves and woodland creatures combined. Better than Mother Teresa took of Calcutta's lepers during her pre-scandal glory years.

The debacle had started with a profile I'd written on one Dr. Frances Wyvern, purportedly a pioneering virologist who excelled at motocross racing and mountain climbing. My research indicated she held a top-level position in the Royal Society, and a MENSA membership. She sounded authentically medical and sporty during our chatty phone interviews. She looked buff and hygienic in the photos she sent. Dr. Frances Wyvern had a Wikipedia page, for God's sake. And a thoroughly convincing British accent. How was I to know that Dr. Wyvern was a total fake?

It turned out Dr. Frances Wyvern was actually Fred Wyckoff, a forty-year-old pharmacist who lived with his mother in a Sacramento suburb. In my twenty-five years as a journalist specializing in the 'unique' profile, I'd never been so thoroughly duped and publicly humiliated. For months I hid out in the den, popping Ativan and watching back-to-back Law and Order reruns. My moods fluctuated between dark and darkest. I was paralyzed in fear that Oprah would come out of retirement and demand to inter-viscerate me. To avoid such a fate, I added Ambien to the Ativan and slept whole days away like a heavily-sedated hibernating bear.

But Dimitri kept me hydrated. He made me chicken soup. He rubbed my feet. He cleaned the house and paid the bills. Eventually he weaned me off my pharmaceutical A friends. He never once said "I told you so" or "It will all be okay." He's still letting it play out with amazing patience, because...honestly? It's far from over. I'm still a basket case.

This dinner party is gonna be a stretch.

Dimitri goes off to shower and shave. I set the table with the clunky ceramic plates we picked up in Guatemala last winter, B.F.W., Before Frances Wyvern. I am not pulling out the good china for Chet. I'll brown-nose only so far. Maybe I'll go frizzy haired, loud and hippy-ish tonight. Don my "This Is What A Feminist Looks Like" t-shirt. If I hadn't already shaved my legs, I'd wear something short and unattractive to compliment my fuzzy shins.

But we need this dinner to go smoothly. Now that I'm unemployable, blacklisted from every major publication, Dimitri's paycheck is all we have. His job at BangleBrains has to last. There's that pesky college tuition to pay, and a crack in our brick façade. Plus, the water heater is acting fickle, the car needs new tires, and, and, and...

I change out the ceramics for the china, and go upstairs for my turn in the shower while there's still enough hot water.

+++++++

"No talking about my former writing career." I have my hair up in a flawless French Twist. I'm wearing a black Donna Karan tunic with black jeans. A bit of mascara and some red lipstick. I look like a well-heeled mime.

"Former?" Dimitri says. We're sitting in the living room, drinking a pre-beer, our traditional warm up, a beer we share before guests arrive and real drinking commences.

"I've decided to stop writing for good. Time for a new career. Maybe I'll become a professional dog walker. It's more lucrative, and it'll get me out of the house."

"Whatevs." Dimitri shrugs and takes a pre-sip.

"Whatevs? You sound like a twelve-year-old girl who adores boy bands. A tween who actually wants to start menstruating."

The doorbell rings. Dimitri thrusts himself up off the couch and lands solidly on two feet, his arms in a wide V. "Let the games begin!" He sprints to the front door as I scurry to the kitchen. I down the rest of the beer by the sink, slurp a swig of water from the faucet, swish it around, and spit to get rid of the yeasty undertones.

When I return to the living room, there's Chet. Everything about him is as thick and shiny as I expected. He's got the kind of hair all men covet, especially men like Dimitri who vainly ignore barbers and hold on to a few pathetic strands that don't even cover their heads. Chet's hair looks as if a small fox has taken residence atop his giant skull, spreading its furry body from ear to ear, all browns and blonds and hints of red.

My husband's new boss is a massive male boulder. He's sweaty, bloated. There's a chance he was handsome once upon a time, with cleft chin and sparkling white teeth, but now he looks like an inflated Disney prince pool float. Veins pop off bowling ball biceps, which squeeze out of the short sleeves of his button-straining shirt, a shirt that does nothing to conceal Chet's sizable gut.

"Helloooo," Chet drawls. He stands spread-legged with that gut thrust forward, unapologetic as he scans my body. His bright blue eyes are otherworldly, turquoise. I assume he's wearing colored contacts. "And who's this sexy lady?" he leers at me, tongue wagging.

Faker, I think. Men like him find women like me as sexy as having their balls waxed. I want to say, "This sexy lady is the kind of lady who wants to puke when she sees you." But I refrain because Chet is Chet. My husband's boss.

"You must be Amanda." A much brighter voice calls from behind the behemoth that is Chet. I crane my neck to look around Chet's mass, and I'm face to face with Chet's 'lady friend' who might possibly be the most beautiful woman I've ever seen. There's something familiar about her, but I can't for the life of me imagine our paths have ever crossed.

"I'm Talulah." She glides gracefully towards me holding out a smooth brown hand. I notice a perfect manicure, big rings, and big knuckles.

I take Talulah's hand, which is cool, and even softer than it looks. Her grip is firm, which I like in another woman; I can't stand it when I shake a woman's hand and she goes all fishy on me. "Nice to meet you Talulah," I say, and mean it. She exudes congeniality, and the more she smiles, the more she reminds me of someone. But I can't place who it is. I know it's someone I like, or liked; however, my addled middle-aged brain is extra fucked by my recent Wyvern-ian breakdown, so forget any recall.

[38]

Instead, I just take her in. Everything on her is long and caramel. Her neck, her arms, her legs. Even her obviously dyed-and-professionally-straightened hair, which goes down to her waist. I can't place her ethnicity. She's about my age, though she's had work done, obviously. Botox and fillers, probably. Rhinoplasty, definitely. Growing up in a suburban Jewish town in the 1970's I can spot a nose job from 100 yards away. I assume Talulah's boobs have been lifted, because, hello, no middle-aged woman has a rack that upright without a little hitch and stitch.

"Your house is amazing," she sighs as she surveys our chotkskes and funky furniture. I hope she doesn't spot the duct tape wrapped around one leg of the coffee table. "You must have used a decorator."

"Nope," I shrug. "We hoarded all this junk on our own."

"May I?" She points to a small majolica vase we have on our mantle. I can't remember where we got it. I'm not even sure I like it anymore.

I nod.

Talulah lifts the vase as if she's handling a newborn baby. "This is far from junk, Amanda." She smiles at me. I smile back. She's restored my faith in the vase. I'm about to ask her if we've met before when Chet interrupts, sidling up to Talulah like a horny cowboy, lassoing her shoulder with his burly arm, which he has to do at an odd angle because she's much taller than he is, especially in her platform sandals.

"Better listen to this gorgeous creature," he says. "She's my art and design advisor. She knows good shit from bad shit. We met last Thursday at The Standard and on the spot I hired her to decorate my new Montauk beach house." Chet rubs Talulah's beautifully toned shoulder as if it's his own cock he's wanking. "Place is gonna be killer."

Talulah smiles tightly. Not the same winning smile I got a moment earlier, before Chet interrupted.

"Yep." Chet can't shut up. "Took me a whole week, but I finally convinced her to go out with me. So, voila! Here we are."

Chet tries to nuzzle Talulah's neck. I'm thinking, ew gross, what is this, middle school? Talulah pushes him off with admirable force, and I breathe an audible sigh of relief.

"Anyone want a drink?" Dimitri says, too loudly.

"Always," Chet blurts.

"We've got wine, beer..."

"What kind of beer?" Chet interrupts.

"Corona?"

Chet wrinkles his nose. "I only drink IPA's. What else ya got?"

Dimitri picks at his forearm hairs. He does this when he's nervous. "Full bar, more or less."

"Bourbon?"

"Sure."

"What kind?"

"Um, I think it's Johnny Walker?"

"Forget it." Chet sighs. "I'll just have some water." He drops his arm from around Talulah. She sways as if she's been released from a body cast.

"Talulah? Anything?" Dimitri asks. He's wincing in preparation for the next line of alcohol interrogation.

"I'll have one of those Coronas, Dimitri," she says. "I only drink Corona."

We all laugh. The three of us, that is, aside from Chet, who's sprawled on the couch with his feet on our coffee table. At least he had the decency to remove his shoes at the front door.

"So Amanda," Chet says, "Dim tells me you're a journalist?"

"Dim does, does Dim?" I sneak a withering glare at my newly (and perhaps aptly-monikered) husband while Chet lurches forward to scoop a fistful of almonds from a bowl on the table.

"Where have I read your stuff?" Chet stuffs the entire stash in his mouth, talking through a static of splintered nut particles.

"Oh, here and there." I'm hoping to leave it at that.

Dimitri has returned with drinks. "Amanda's profiles have been in The Atlantic, The New Republic, Ms. magazine," He can't help himself. He's my cheerleader even when I explicitly tell him not to be. "You might remember her New Yorker profile on Boutros Boutros-Ghali."

"Whosa Whosa WhaWha?" Chet mimics.

"He was the Secretary General of the United Nations in the 90's, Chet," says Talulah. She turns to me and smiles. "I remember that piece. I loved how you compared Ghali's Rwandan connections to your Aunt Sadie's relationship with the saleswomen at Loehmann's."

I'm speechless. It's been a while since anyone has complimented my writing. After the Wyvern scandal, all I got were accusations of being a hack.

"I've loved everything you've written," Talulah continues as she settles her gorgeous body on the couch next to Chet. "When Chet invited me to have dinner with his new legal counsel and his wife, the journalist Amanda Lowenstein, how could I resist?" She pats Chet on the knee and smiles at him sexily, manipulatively. Using something I've never accessed in my own lady-body: feminine wiles. It works. Chet seems to melt like butter on my couch. He's quiet, for the moment. Talulah turns back to me and says, "I died over your hilarious deconstruction of the Monkees in Ms. back in the late 90's."

"I can't believe you read that," I finally speak. Chet's lady friend knows about my Ghali article, and even more so, my feminist take on the original boy band. I'm turning red. My cheeks are hot.

"'Keep Davy. I Wanted Mike Nesmith's Baby'. Oh. My. God. Hysterical!" Talulah throws her head back and laughs a big gutsy laugh. Once again I'm struck with that I-know-you-where-did-you-come-from-you-wonderful-woman feeling.

"Are you working on anything new?" Talulah asks.

"New?" I squeak. My heart is beating cardiac arrest fast. The antiperspirant I caked into the crevices of my armpits is proving useless. Streams of sweat travel down my torso to the top of my tasteful, classy mime pants.

Everyone waits for me to answer Talulah's seemingly benign question. New? I haven't so much as typed a "please unsubscribe" email or a "TTYL" text since the Wyvern debacle. Chet glares at me like Pablo Escobar eying a Colombian snitch. Dimitri looks panicked, rubbing his bald spot as if it's a bottle and a genie might appear if he keeps at it long enough. Talulah however, is all sweetness, patience and light.

Finally I talk. "Dogs," I say. "Dogs in the Olive Garden."

Dimitri gapes at me, drop-jawed, with a what-the-fuck-are-you-talking-about expression.

I can't help myself. It's free association time. "How fast food restaurants are moving to accommodate our pet-crazy society to increase sales," I continue. "The need for commercial service industries to address the uptick in domestic animal ownership."

[43]

"That sounds fascinating," says Talulah.

"I have a dog," says Chet, as if he's announced winning the Prix de Rome.

"How wonderful!" I cry, as if Chet has won the Prix de Rome. "What kind of dog?"

"Dunno," Chet shrugs. "Labradoodle? Cockapoodle? Cockador?"

Talulah frowns. "How can you not know what kind of dog you have?"

Chet shrugs again. He's good at shrugging. "I just got it, like, last summer."

Note: It is now, once again, summer.

"She's a great dog, though," Chet continues. "Cute as a button. Only barks when I get too close to her, so like, there's not a whole lot of petting going on. But the dog walker tells me she gets along great with all the other mutts at the dog run. I picked her cause she's hypoallergenic. She doesn't shed, so I can have guests in any part of my apartment." Now he leers at Talulah. "Even the bedroom."

Talulah smirks and takes a long draw from her Corona.

"She sounds great, Chet," Dimitri says cheerily, like Mr. Rogers talking to preschool viewers. "What's her name?"

Chet pauses. He has to think.

"You've got to be kidding," Talulah says under her breath.

[44]

"Bingo!" Chet finally announces.

"Bingo, as in you remember, or Bingo as in her name...oh?" I ask.

"Her name. Cute, right?" Chet is very pleased with himself.

"Adorable," I say then I turn to Talulah. "Would you like a lime for your Corona? Dim, you forgot Talulah's lime. I'll go get some."

"Can you please stop calling me that," Dimitri says under his breath as I pass him on my way to the kitchen.

"Whatevs," I say back.

When I return with cut lime and almonds to refill the nut bowl, Chet is telling a story about a recent trip he'd taken somewhere far away and exotic.

"The view from my cabana was fucking insane! Looking out over the fucking South China Sea. I mean, for fucking real!"

"Sounds fucking wonderful, Chet," says Talulah in an admirable deadpan. She gingerly squeezes a slice of lime into her bottle and takes another long draw.

"I tell you, the natives couldn't have been sweeter. You'd think that they'd hate Americans, I mean, we've raped that country. Literally raped it. Poor schmucks don't have a pot to piss in, but they're still smiling all the time. And the women come up to you, offering you, well..." He looks at Talulah, then over at me and smirks. "Maybe I shouldn't talk about that in mixed company."

"Maybe not," Talulah says as she looks at me and rolls her eyes so quick and subtly I almost miss it, but just almost. We're comrades, me and this glamorous creature, in spite of our stylistic differences and our taste in men.

"Well then," I clap-clap my hands. "I'll get dinner started. You all sit here and relax."

"Let me help you," Talulah gets up. Chet reaches towards her, but she's too quick. She's around the coffee table in no time, maneuvering like a quarterback to escape his grabby hands.

Normally I'd rebuff her offer. I hate people in the kitchen with me. I find it incredibly distracting. They want to chat, and thoughts fly out of my head while the beans burn, or I turn the burner on under the pasta pot forgetting there's no water in it yet, or I dress the salad with vinegar only. But maybe Talulah needs to get away from Chet and his off-the-charts racist, sexist, bigoted ways as much as I do, so I say, "That'd be great!"

Before I know it, we're in the kitchen together, and I'm letting Talulah slice the olives for my pasta dish.

"Can you imagine what life is like for that poor dog?" she asks.

"He seems very fond of her."

"Yeah, right," Talulah is chopping the olives. She starts to sing, "There was an asshole had a dog and Bingo was her name-o."

We both laugh.

[46]

I really want to ask her, what's a nice girl like you doing with a douche like him, even if it is just a first date. But instead I go with, "So what's it like working with Chet?"

"Impossible," she sighs. "But he's got money to burn, which is an art consultant's dream." She's chopping at weed-wacker pace and her jaw seems tight. "Honestly? I need this gig. I'm in a financial hole."

"Ah," I sigh, "I know about financial holes."

"I mean, let's be real. Chet's a bore, right?"

Chet is my husband's boss. Talulah is his date. His 'lady friend'. Clearly not his girlfriend. Yet. Still, maybe she's setting me up somehow? "You could say that," I nod, trying to keep it tame.

Talulah stares at me with gorgeous deep brown, heavily mascara-ed eyes. She's about to say something else when Dimitri appears at the kitchen door.

"Um, Amanda, where'd you put Emmett's old guitar?"

"In the back of his closet, behind all those book's he's never going to read again but refuses to let me get rid of. Why?"

"Chet wrote a song he wants to play for us," Dimitri is sporting a fakey-fake smile. "Once I get the guitar and he's ready, can you two come back to the living room?"

"No prob," I say, turning the burner off and making a note to myself to turn it back on when I'm allowed back in the kitchen.

"Great," Dimitri says and dashes away in search of the guitar. It's then when I finally get to ask Talulah, "You seem so familiar to me. Have we ever met before?"

Talulah looks worried. She pauses and it's clear she's making some kind of bargain with her own psyche. Then, presto chango! She flashes me one of her cover girl smiles and says, "I'm not sure. Maybe." She hands me the chopped and ready olives.

"Thanks," I say as I dump the olives into a big bowl. I'd ask Talulah more, but I'm so cautious I'm like the conversational equivalent of a concrete slab. We chop and dice in awkward silence for a moment when finally Dimitri calls from the living room.

"Come on in, Girls. Chet's ready."

"Oh Lordy," Talulah fans herself as if she's in a non-air-conditioned subway car. "This is gonna be a trip."

Chet is sitting upright, tuning my eldest son's semi-forgotten guitar. Dimitri is back to forearm hair-plucking, which is slightly less annoying than scalp rubbing. Talulah sits next to Chet, but with more of a gap between them than before. I remain standing with a wooden spoon in my hand, trying to look like a gourmet chef who needs to get back to work as soon as possible.

Chet clears his throat. He proceeds to sing a song that is a mishmash of guttural calls, and whistles. He hums, and then blurts incomprehensible phrases that sound like a blend of Yiddish and Portuguese. He nods his cleft chin, the fox-like hair flops in his eyes. All the while he's thumping his hand on the side of the guitar, barely strumming the strings. When he's done, Chet is gauging our reactions. He's eager and expectant, like my sons used to be after they played mediocre pee-wee soccer on D-list teams.

I am so overwhelmed with Chet's display of dreck that if I try to talk I'll break down in hysterics. I can see out of the corner of my eye that Talulah seems to be in a similar state.

My brave husband rises to the occasion. "Wow," Dimitri says, "That was, ah, some song."

"Thanks, Dim," Chet places the guitar string-side down on the coffee table, leans back against the couch cushions, and yawns. "It comes from a really raw place. Deep, man, really deep. Kinda takes it out of me. But I guess that's what being creative is all about. Amanda, as a writer you'd know about that, right?"

I'm past the hysterics, but still not capable of safe verbal exchange. All I can do is grin. I probably look like a demented jack-o'-lantern.

Talulah pats Chet's knee. "Bravo, Maestro!" She turns to me. "We'd better get back to work, Amanda."

As she rises, Chet gives her a slap on the ass. Talulah's face darkens and she looks like she's going to turn around and deck him. But she doesn't. She's back to glamour and sweetness in a blink of an eye. Together, she and I saunter away.

+++++++

"Okay then," I say as cheerily as possible when we're back in the kitchen. "Where were we?"

Talulah's taken a fierce stance, both hands on her hips. "That stuff about the people in the Philippines? Natives? That shit about the women offering sex? Fuck that."

I envy her defined triceps. I worked on my triceps many moons ago during three complimentary personal training sessions I got as a sign on bonus at my gym. I assume my triceps are still there, hiding somewhere under my saggy upper arm flesh.

"So it was the Philippines Chet was describing," I turn the burner on for the pasta water. And yes, I remember to fill the pot also. "I was wondering where he'd been. Sounds like he enjoyed himself."

"Chet's an asshole," she says.

"Not the most tactful guy I've ever met." I'm still trying to be Switzerland.

"That song?" she cries. "Like a bad SNL skit."

It is really hard not to join her on the Chet-bashing train.

"And that jerk slapped my ass. Without asking! I don't mind a bit of slapping when it's consensual. That was a very non-consensual slap."

"Now where did I put the balsamic?" This may be more information than I'm prepared to digest. I start opening and shutting cabinet doors.

"Come on, Amanda. This isn't like you."

How would she know what I'm like? When I risk a quick glance back I find Talulah staring at me, like she knows me, like really knows me.

"Whaddya mean?" I squeak. I'm Jiminy Cricket, jumping around the kitchen like an insect.

"Okay. Time to get real," she says. "You weren't like this in college."

"Aha!" I stop hopping and stare back at Talulah. "So we have met. We went to college together."

She nods. "I remember you walking past Fraternity Row flashing your tits, giving the finger to cat-calling frat boys hanging off their balconies."

I did that. For real.

"DREAM ON, CRETINS. YOU'LL NEVER GET A HOLD OF THESE." Talulah grabs her own much-nicer boobs in homage to my favorite college rant.

I blush. "Did we, um, hang out?" I feel bad I don't remember her, because clearly she remembers me.

"Not so much. Just a bit," she sighs. "I was very different back then."

"Weren't we all?" I sigh too, and for a moment we're quiet, sharing a moment, remembering our younger idealistic selves, girls who called themselves women, braless, hairy, fearless, gorgeous creatures who could and would have sex with anyone they chose, who protested wars, unfair labor practices, who rallied for freedom of speech, who played guitars and zithers and danced topless whenever they could.

"Alright, I've been trying to find the right time to lay this on you, so here it comes." Her mouth is a taut lipstick line, her eyes are dark and steady. "You might remember me as Thomas."

Talulah stares at me. And then I start to see her, or rather, him. Thomas, a thin graceful guy who hung out with a bunch of Semiotics snobs, a clique I wasted half of sophomore year trying to break into. Thomas smoked Gitanes like the rest of them. He wore a flamboyant paisley silk scarf around his neck. He did entire London Times Sunday Crossword puzzles without any hesitation. I think he played the piccolo. He stayed on the edge of their pretentious parade by choice, while I desperately wanted to march along, waving my copy of Barthes *A Lover's Discourse*, or singing the praises of Derrida. Mostly I remember Thomas was the only one in that clique who paid any attention to me.

Thomas had been best friends with Lars, a waspishly gorgeous blond god I had a hopeless crush on. But I was invisible to Lars. He only had eyes for Sarah, a ruling class pothead with a horsey overbite and ties to the Rockefellers.

But Lars is beside the point. It's Talulah who matters, Talulah who grins at me now. I definitely remember this smile. The only difference is thirty years ago there wasn't a smooth coating of coral lipstick highlighting the openness, or lack of pretense.

"Thomas!" I can't believe it, but I can. "Holy shit!" Talulah puts a finger to her lips.

"Ohhh," I whisper, "Chet."

She nods.

"He doesn't know."

"Obviously," she smirks. "Hey do you remember that party where you and I talked about Petticoat Junction for hours?"

And then it comes back to me, a glorious flash of nostalgia. A smoke-filled sparsely-furnished off campus apartment. Nina Simone on the stereo. Gesticulating post-pubescent know-it-alls mingling about. Thomas and I were happy schlumped on a saggy couch talking unironically about Petticoat Junction. No deconstructing, no analyzing. No Derrida-ing. Just a couple of fangirls, as we would now be called, gushing about the Jo's; Betty, Bobbie, and Billie. Toot, toot.

I take her in. "How long have you..." I falter, "when...how..." I sound like an idiot. I'm cool with all sorts of gender variables, I am, but this is Thomas from college! Thomas! And he-she is kind of, sort of, dating my husband's boss!

"I've known I was Talulah since the day I was born. But this..." she traces a long line from her left shoulder to her right hip, as if she's drawing a beauty queen's sash, "this has been a work in progress for the last five years."

"You look amazing."

She flicks a wrist and rolls her eyes. "You're too sweet."

"No. Seriously. You're so fucking gorgeous, I can't stand it."

She shrugs. "Alright. You win. I am."

"What a coincidence," I squealed. "You coming here tonight."

"Well it's one thing we can thank Chet for. I couldn't pass up the opportunity to see you again. I've been following your writing for years. I always said: Amanda Lowenstein is gonna do something important."

"Who'd you say that to?"

"Oh, all those self-important creeps. Lars, Andrew, that bitch Betsy, Stoner Sarah."

I feel a sense of accomplishment I haven't felt in months. Years. Decades.

"You really got a bum rap on that Frances Wyvern thing," Talulah says.

I shake and hang my head. "No. I deserved it. I fucked up. I got lazy."

Talulah grabs me by the shoulders. "Listen. Take it from a former faker. When someone wants to pretend they're something they're not, if they work hard enough they can fool anyone. That sad little man who led you to believe he was a fantastic woman? Guaranteed

[54]

somewhere inside that guy, that's who he is. But his insides don't match his outsides. And you got caught in the in-between." Her grip is strong, guy strong. I think how marvelous it would be to have her kind of physical strength, her kind of beauty. But mostly her kind of bravery.

I'm suddenly exhausted so I lean forward and turn my head to rest my cheek on Talulah's chest. "Nice pair," I sigh. "Mine are like two partially deflated Aerobeds."

Talulah chuckles and my cheek bounces on her fantastic, if somewhat fabricated, firmness.

"We should've hung out more in college," I sigh.

"That's for damn sure," she says.

"We could hang out now?" I offer.

"That's for damn sure," she repeats.

I lift my head and look up at her face. Her eyebrows are so beautifully shaped. Maybe she'll take me for a makeover? I could use a makeover. "So, pardon my ignorance. But how does it work? Do you tell guys? Will you tell Chet?"

"It depends. Some I tell, some I don't. Because," she lets go of my shoulders, and points to her crotch. "I haven't done the ultimate yet."

"You still have a...a..."

"Oh yeah," she drawls. "And it's a nice package. I'm gonna be sad when it's gone. But only kind of sad. Meanwhile I've decided I'm gonna shock the shit out of our friend Chet tonight. Get him all riled up, then whip it

[55]

out and wipe the smug smile off that pompous sucka." She does the sassy head lolling thing that only a woman as majestic as her can pull off without looking like an idiot.

"But what about the Montauk job? What if Chet fires you? What about your financial hole?"

"Amanda, really." Talulah shakes her head. "We may be a couple of old biddies, but we've still got to challenge the patriarchy when we can. Even if it means we lose a chunk of change. Misogynistic dickwad fighting. That's the real job."

"There is a God!" I stage-whisper and shake both fists victoriously. "But be careful. He's a big guy."

"Ah," she waves a hand dismissively. "I can take him down with one hand tied behind my back if I have to."

And I believe her. "You have to call me tomorrow and give me all the details."

After we exchange phone numbers, we get back to work, boiling pasta, kitchen girl talk, catching up on grown up lives.

Dimitri pops his head through the kitchen door just as we're putting on the finishing touches.

"Everything okay in here?" he asks.

"Right as rain," I say with a smile.

"How much longer until we eat? Chet's got low blood sugar, and says if he doesn't eat soon he might faint or something."

[56]

"Is that a promise?" Talulah asks.

Dimitri is at a loss for words.

"Don't worry, Dim," I say, "She's one of us. Dinner will be ready in five. Meanwhile tell Chet to chew on these," I gently lob a bag of carrots in Dimitri's direction.

Dimitri catches the carrots then glances at Talulah. She is, of course, smiling. Dimitri looks relieved and confused at the same time. He leaves with the bag of carrots swinging in his hand while Talulah and I finish our preparations.

When we're done, I follow Talulah to the dining room with bowls and platters of goodness. I think how we might've been fearless back in the day but we were also pretty ignorant, and blind. We had secrets. Now we're wiser. Braver. Or at least Talulah is.

Me? I've still got some learning to do. But as I watch my new friend sashay ahead of me, as I admire her perfect (dare I say, slap-worthy) ass I think: Let the dogs walk themselves. She's arrived, she's the real thing, and I have a new profile to write.

Snow Day!

Kristin:

The kids were already getting on Kristin's nerves, and they'd only been in the car for five minutes.

"Mommeeee," whined Larissa. "Jordan is kicking me."

"Am not."

"Am too."

"Am not, you stupid."

"MOMMEEE! Jordan called me stupid."

A rustling in the backseat. An audible inhale. An ear-piercing wail.

"She bit me," cried Jordan. "Mom, look." A scrawny arm speared forward, obstructing Kristin's view out the snow-speckled windshield.

"Jordan, I'm driving. Buckle up and get back in your seat."

The only way to get through the 20-minute trip home would be lots of snacks. Kristin had come prepared with individually-wrapped packs of organic gummy bears and antioxidant-enriched vegan granola bars in a recyclable shopping bag on the seat next to her.

"Here," she tossed two of each into the back seat of the Escalade. "Treats for my sweets."

"These suck," said Jordan, tossing his bag of gummy bears back into the front. "I hate these."

"Me too. They taste like poo-poo." agreed Larissa, whose aim was worse, or better, accidentally/on purpose socking her mother gummily in the back of the skull.

"Excuse me?" Kristin struggled to keep her voice calm but firm. "We do NOT speak that way in this family, and we do NOT throw our food."

Kristin was a tad on edge. Why hadn't she been invited to the 3 p.m. board meeting? She'd been planning her debut for months, the surprise introduction by Craig as his choice for new CFO at TechBros. Tada, here's Kristin, ready to take the bull, or cow, or sow by the horns.

But no. Instead Craig had made his stupid "Snow Day" announcement at 2 p.m. Everyone at TechBros had the rest of the afternoon off. The younger employees raced to the elevators in their recycled jeans and Doc Martens, piled into Mini-Coopers and Priuses, heading west, back to Brooklyn, to railroad apartments, craft beers, and Scrabble nights.

Kristin should have high-tailed it east to Brookdale, but she'd stayed at her desk, paralyzed, as the office emptied. The board meeting was all she'd prepared for. All she'd wanted.

"Krissie," called Craig as he bounded puppy-style past her at 2:15, on his way to the fourth-floor boardroom, no doubt. "What are you still doing here? Go! Get home and get cozy before the snow starts to fuck everything up."

"What about the board meeting?" Kristin asked.

"Cancelled," Craig lied. He couldn't even look her in the eye. "So go on. Git."

Lying creepazoid. Dumbo Craig with his big ears and goofy grin. Repulsive slime-bucket. The only reason he was CEO was because he'd gone to Harvard with Justin, wunderkind creator and chief programmer at TechBros. Both guys were just that, guys. Not even men. Young boys club. Barely out of diapers.

Kenneth:

Once the hooker exited the passenger side, Kenneth settled his big-bellied body in to the smooth leather driver's seat of his Lexus.

Thank God for heated seats, he thought as he pressed the new-fangled non-key key against the dashboard to magically start the engine. Instantly his tush and back felt the glow. This car, with its slick beauty and instant gratifications, was worth every cent.

So was Adele. Annette. Or whatever her name was. His penis was still happily throbbing. He'd paid $200. And that, too, had been worth every cent.

Kenneth loved his life. At least this part. At least momentarily. The heated seat, his spent-but-still-twitchy cock, the warm cocoon and humming purr of the brand new Lexus LS. How could he savor this, make it last? He sat with the engine running—screw the environmentalists—and shut his eyes. Kenneth soaked in his debauchery like a fat cube of French bread dipped in a warm fondue of melted gruyere.

When he opened his eyes a few minutes later, big wet snowflakes were falling, melting the moment they landed on the windshield. How goddamn spectacular, thought Kenneth. Nothing like a harmless dusting to make a guy feel at one with nature.

All the whiteness and purity juxtaposed his sullied perversions. Jarred him out of his post-ejaculation reverie. He thought: I'm a married man, a father, a grandfather for Christ's sake, paying for blowjobs from barely-legals in abandoned corporate parking lots. The shame came on then like it always did, this time catching Kenneth in the solar plexus, causing a knot, a lurch, and the release of an explosive burp.

Kenneth adjusted his ample body and begrudgingly fastened his seatbelt. How he longed for the good old days when they were a choice, not a legal obligation. He drove out of the parking lot and made his way towards the LIE.

Within ten minutes, the snow was no longer pretty. It pummeled his car with punishing icy pellets. Kenneth couldn't see for shit.

Kyle:

Kyle downed the last spitty sip of his fourth Heineken. He checked his slowly-dying phone, pretending he'd gotten a message, but really he was just checking the time. It was 2 p.m. He'd been at Brian's house for two hours. More losers had just arrived, strung-out tweakers from Bay Shore, douchebags with permanent paranoia.

It was time for Kyle to split. Aside from the addition of these Bay Shore lowbrows, Brittany DeMarco was drunken face-sucking her bouncer-build boyfriend on the couch across from Kyle. It drove him batshit crazy. Brittany had barely changed in the six years since high school. She still had that donkey hee-haw laugh and that killer smile. Kyle would always remember that one time, end of junior year behind the 7-11, when something had almost happened between them. Almost. With Brittany DeMarco, almost meant not ever. Not even in your fucking dreams.

Kyle stood to leave and realized he was mondo sauced, definitely operating with softened edges. He raised his hand to say goodbye, but why bother? No one was paying any attention.

When he opened the front door he lost his footing and got hit with a shockfest of wind and snow. He slammed the door shut. The TV weather wonks had said the big storm wasn't going to hit Long Island until after 8 p.m. So what the hell was this? No way Kyle could make the walk back home. His leather jacket would get ruined. He didn't have a hat. He was wearing his Converse.

There was only one thing to do. Borrow Brian's car and bring it back to him tomorrow. No way Brian would miss it. The only thing Brian was going to possibly need in the next 24 hours was a cold shower, or his stomach pumped.

Kyle grabbed Brian's car keys from Brian's 'everything bowl,' a high school football helmet turned upside down and lined with tinfoil. Kyle steeled himself, opened the front door a second time, and pushed through the wind and snow towards Brian's tricked-out Cutlass.

Kyle's face felt like a giant Slushie. Once in the driver's seat, he swatted snow from the work-in-progress beard growing on his chin, and brushed as much as he could off his jacket, but still snow melted its way down the back of his neck in a long teasing tickle. His Converse were sopping wet. He might as well have run to the car barefoot.

Kyle looked out the windshield at big wet flakes melting the moment they landed on the glass. If snow didn't fuck everything up, it would be really cool, in a nature-ish kind of way. But snow was generally a royal pain in the butt. Good thing the drive home was only a couple of miles. He'd be there in no time.

Kenneth:

Kenneth wondered if Lorraine would be glad to have him home early. More importantly, he wondered what she'd whip up for dinner. The night before, she'd served some nice lamb chops, mashed potatoes, and creamed spinach, with leftover birthday cake from earlier in the day, when they'd hosted an eighth year birthday party for crybaby Corey, fourth grandson in a line of little pansies. Too bad Kenneth's four daughters had all married idiots and made mostly idiot kids. A bunch of moochers. None of them lived in houses big enough to host their own kids' birthday parties.

Kenneth was sick of being the Grand Pooba, the big boss, the grandaddy of all granddaddies. At home, at work. It was the same tiresome story. Everyone wanted a piece of him. At least Corey's party provided Kenneth with an excuse for some early afternoon drinking. And that leftover cake.

[65]

His guess was Lorraine would be restrictive tonight, in counterpoint to yesterday's excesses. Probably would serve him an underdressed salad and a poached piece of fish. No cake, just a couple of Vanilla Wafers for dessert. She took good care of him, but only in the food department, Lorraine did. Food and mindless chatter. That was about it these days.

The sign for the entrance to the expressway was barely visible, but Kenneth knew this route like he knew the liver-spotted back of his hand. Jesus, the snow was really coming down, though. He'd have to take it slower. There was barely anyone else on the road. He saw a white SUV, an Escalade that was like an Abominable Snowman, dangerously camouflaged. The monster car was careening all over the goddamn place, no doubt being driven by some young a-hole overcompensating for what he lacked in his shorts. Cretin was going to get someone killed.

Where were all the other cars? Kenneth wondered. It's just snow, not terrorism or a goddamn hurricane. Well, let the pussies stay off the roads if they wanted. More room for me.

Kenneth steered the Lexus on to the blank expanse of highway. The lane lines were gone, coated in slick whiteness. But Kenneth prided himself on his stellar driving skills. He held his steering wheel and peered out like a ship's captain navigating an open sea.

Kristin:

"Why did you pick us up today and not Daddy?" asked Jordan. "You're supposed to be at work."

"Yay-ah," Larissa whined in, "Daddy always picks us up. You're always at your job."

"Well, that's not entirely true, Sweetie," Kristin grit her teeth and veered around a blue car with tacky racing stripes that was going, like, 2 miles an hour. She bulldozed her way up the eastbound entrance to the expressway. "Mommy picks you up every now and then."

"I guess..." Larissa kicked the back of the passenger seat in a relentless rhythm. Thump, thump...thump. Thump, thump...thump.

"Where's Daddy?" asked Jordan.

"Daddy's home waiting for us." Watching internet porn. Or taking a nap, thought Kristin. "Larissa, stop kicking the seat, please."

The expressway was a ghost road. Aside from the snailmobile she'd passed at the entrance, Kristin saw only one other car, a black Lexus driving in a straight and steady line. She came up on it, and took a nice leftward edge around, gunning her massive engine and leaving the Lexus in a blur of snow dust. She wondered if her unemployed deadbeat husband still kept a secret stash of bourbon hidden behind Jordan's soccer gear in the garage. She just might need to indulge. Park the car, prod-shoo-shove the kids inside, let Daddy take off their wet, sloppy boots and damp jackets. Let him clean off their sticky faces and grubby hands while she self-fortified.

It was snowing with a vengeance. The Escalade whipped and skidded over unplowed mounds of snow. Really, couldn't the Highway Department get their act together and do a little plowing?

Larissa was still kicking the seat.

"Larissa, I asked you nicely to stop doing that. If you don't stop you'll get a time out when we get home."

"But I'm not doing the same song. I'm doing another song," Larissa cried. Thump, thump...thumpthumpthump...thump.

"No whining. Use your nice voice, Lar-"

Kristin stopped talking as the car did a complete 360, then skidded to a stop. The entire front end of the car hood wedged deep in a snow drift.

"Weheee," giggled Jordan. "Just like Great Adventure!"

Kyle:

How could so much snow fall so quickly? Kyle thought that it was as if God was taking a giant white dump. Or dumping all his celestial blow. Maybe Mrs. God had given him the ultimatum: No more coke for you, God or I'm out of Heaven. Gonna go live with the kids on, on...on Cloud Nine!

Kyle chuckled. He cracked himself up all the time. Maybe he would nix his plan to go to audio engineering school and try stand-up comedy instead. How cool would that be? He imagined himself up on the stage at Jones Beach. Brittany DeMarco would be his girlfriend, of course. She'd be sitting in the VIP section right under the stage staring up at him, laughing at his brilliant jokes. From his perch in front of the mike, he would take a quick peek down to see her smiling face and the sweet upper mounds of those great tits. How hot would that life be?

Speaking of mounds, there were mounds of snow everywhere. The streets were a mess. And Brian's Cutlass kept losing traction. Those racing stripes he'd painted on the sides were a joke. The crap car had barely any power.

The expressway might be in better shape than the surface roads. Kyle would have to make a big loop around, but it would get him back to his own house— actually his mother's house—where he planned to spend the rest of the day watching a lot of Comedy Central. Pick up a few tips from the pros. Start working on his own routine.

He drove slowly towards the entrance. Just as he was thinking how there were no other cars anywhere, a big-ass white Escalade almost rear-ended him before veering out from behind and gunning it on to the expressway in a ghostly blur.

Sweet ride, thought Kyle. But the lucky SOB better tone down the NASCAR routine or he's gonna end up dead.

If Kyle made it big on the stand-up comedy circuit, he might buy himself an SUV. But not the Escalade. Too pimpmobile. Too Russian mobster. The SUV Kyle really dug was the Denali. The Denali was classy. Understated. The kind of car a humble celebrity would drive. Plus, white was a stupid non-color for a car. Kyle would go with silver, or forest green, or red.

Yeah, red, he decided. Most def.

Kenneth:

Things turned mighty nasty by the time Kenneth passed Exit 60, the sign for which he could barely read through the deep white curtain. The Lexus was sliding like a greased pig on an icy pond. No traction, no visibility, nada. If he could just make it to Exit 62, he would be in like Flynn, home five minutes later with his feet up on his ottoman and TV tray wedged across his belly.

Kenneth burped again. Enough of this, he thought. He'd been gassy since before the blowjob, and he'd hoped that getting sucked off would alleviate his stomach woes. Sometimes blowjobs did wonders for other systems in his old machine. Gut issues. Headaches. Back pain. But not this time. No magic cure from the lips and tongue of Adele, or Andrea, or Amy, or whatever-her-name-was. Plus his seat belt was so tight it was cutting off the circulation in his left arm.

The snow was so unforgiving he'd almost not seen the white Escalade pressed up against a snowdrift in the breakdown lane of the HOV. Kenneth continued driving. Serves the asshole right for driving a nearly invisible car like a fucking commando, he thought. No doubt the idiot has a fancy cellphone. He can call his wife, or one of his young buck buddies, and they can come get his sorry ass. I'm on my way home to poached fish and the Golf Channel.

He'd barely made it 50 yards when his conscience got the better of him. He had to help. Besides, maybe if he saved the Escalade-driving asshole it would serve as penance for getting blown by what's-her-name. Cancel out today's sin. Clean his slate, temporarily.

Kenneth pulled over to the HOV breakdown lane. He put the Lexus in reverse, and shifted to look over his shoulder and begin the backward trip to salvation. But the seatbelt wouldn't stretch. It cut in, causing a sharper pain.

"Goddamn piece of shit seat belt," he cursed out loud, fumbling to unclasp the buckle, hoping with more mobility he'd be able to navigate backwards clearly. But clear sight was impossible. Kenneth reversed into whiteness, blinder than blind.

[71]

Kristin:

"Oh. Great," Kristin grunted. "Just. Perfect." Every attempt she made to move the Escalade caused the tires to spin uselessly. The snow continued to pile up on the hood of her car, thick, white, without pity.

"Mommee," whined Jordan. "I'm hungry."

"Me too," Larissa joining in. Of course. Not an original bone in her younger sibling body.

"Here." Kristin picked up the shopping bag of snacks and tossed the entire thing backwards, half-heartedly aiming for the space between her two car-seated children, but if she whacked one of them by accident, so be it.

"Momeeee. I told you. I don't like these snacks. I want good snacks."

"Yeah. These are poopy sna-"

"SHUT THE HELL UP! BOTH OF YOU! OR I'LL THROW YOU OUT INTO THE FUCKING BLIZZARD! DO YOU HEAR ME?"

For a brief moment all was peaceful in Kristin's oversized fortress of glass and steel. She took a deep breath and closed her eyes. I'm fine. I'm stellar, even if that fuckhead-piece-of-shit-pencildick Craig doesn't think so.

Peaceful, until Larissa started to mewl like a tortured kitten.

Kristin relented and turned around to take Larissa's grubby little hand. Where were those sani-wipes?

Larissa's mewling subsided just as the black Lexus drove past.

"Thank fucking God!" cried Kristin.

But the Lexus moved on without hesitation. The faint reddish blur of taillights faded to near nothingness.

"Oh shit," Kristin wailed. "Please, nooooo! Come back!"

"Mommy," Jordan whispered. "You really shouldn't say so many naughty words."

Kristin would have to call Triple A and insist they get someone to her immediately. If not, she would be forced to call her lazy-ass husband and demand he get one of his deadbeat friends to pull or lift or tow her out of this catastrophe.

Then she saw the white reverse lights of the Lexus. Inching ever closer. Coming back to save her. She loved the driver already.

Kenneth:

Even with the belt unbuckled Kenneth was in pain. In fact, the pain was excruciating. Fucking unbearable. Kenneth had to stop driving. He shifted into park. A prickly heat at the center of his chest spread across his shoulder and radiated down his left arm. He was short of breath. He was dizzy. He was nauseous.

Kristin:

The Lexus just sat there, so close to Kristin, yet so far.

"Why did you stop?" she called out.

"You asked me to stop, Momeee," Larissa snuffled. "I'm being a good girl. No kicking and no whining."

"I'm not talking to you, Sweetie," Kristin said through gritted teeth.

"But I'm being good too," added Jordan. "Really good. Like really, really good."

"I'm not talking to you either, Jordan. Now shush. Both of you. Mommy needs to concentrate."

"I should get, like, five gold stars on my rewards chart when we get home," Jordan continued.

"Well I should get like ten hundreds." Torturers, both of them.

"Well I should get fifty million trillion." Unending.

"Well I should get one thousand thousand." Like the goddamn snow.

"That's less than fifty million trillion, so I win you dumbo," Jordan declared.

[74]

Kristin put her head down on the steering wheel and moaned.

Kyle:

Nothing worked in Brian's junkheap car. It wouldn't do more than 10 mph, the heat was a joke, the windshield wipers had only one mucho-retardo setting, the clock was broken, and the radio only picked up one snoozefest news station from which, at least, Kyle learned that he was driving in 'The Storm of the Century,' that 'an unforeseen shift in cold fronts had stalled what had been expected to be a moderate snowstorm, turning it in to a locally-lethal blizzard'. Roads were closed all over Suffolk County as of 3 p.m.

Without a working dashboard clock, and a dead-as-a-roach-in-a-roach-motel cellphone, Kyle had no idea what time it was. Probably only like 2:30. He'd be home soon enough. Or maybe not, at the rate he was going.

Kristin:

It had been five minutes since the Lexus had almost come to save them. Kristin could see the Lexus' parking lights illuminated, and exhaust coming from the tailpipe. Was it possible the driver was waiting for them to get out and trek way over there?

"Kids, you stay here. Mommy needs to go see if that nice car up ahead is going to give us a ride home."

"Can't we come?" asked Jordan. "I'm bored."

"No. You can't. Do not under any circumstances get out of your seats or you will both get timeouts when we get home. Do you hear me?"

"Whatever," Jordan said, like a jaded fifteen-year-old. Kristin should revert to the old ways, and wash his mouth out with soap. Like her own mother used to do. Once this snow debacle was over and she had her 'Mom at Home' clothes on, she would grab a bar of Ivory and go to town on that little brat's tongue.

But now she needed to focus on the Lexus. She forced her car door open and stepped out in to white oblivion.

Kenneth:

He knew what this was. He was having a heart attack. Dr. Schlossberg had warned Kenneth this might happen if he didn't cut back on the booze, food, and cigars.

Kenneth tried not to panic. He concentrated on the snow, willed it to be beautiful to him. He struggled to hold on to an old memory of his daughters going girl-giddy with excitement playing in the stuff, sticking out tongues to catch flakes as if they were taking wafers at communion.

But then he saw what's-her-name's tongue. Angie-Ameila-Annie. Today's fall from grace. He was bombarded with too many thoughts of too many tongues. Too many crossed wires, too many melded memories punishing him. Punching him in the chest.

Kenneth sat as bolt upright as a fat man having a coronary could. "What a fool," he cried. "I am such a fucking fool."

The pain was searing, pitiless, like the goddamn, ugly blizzard. And then the pain ended, and everything went black.

But the snow continued.

Kristin:

Kristin gathered the collar of her cream-colored cashmere coat around her throat and trudged through the snow, wearing textured hose and four-inch heels. She could barely feel her legs from the knees down.

She got to the Lexus and peered in the passenger side window. A fat older guy sat in the driver's seat, his jowls spreading over the collar of his overcoat, his head tilted forward.

Taking a nap? she wondered, I mean, now? Really? Kristin tapped on the window. Be polite, but persistent, she coached herself. And if all else fails, offer him money.

Not that it looked like this guy needed money. He was driving the Lexus LS. Top of the line. Craig Shit-for-brains bought himself the very same model after TechBros went public the previous year. Like that little twerp really needed another car. He had at least ten. Toys, all of them.

Kristin rapped again, louder this time. The snoozing old geezer wasn't waking up. She slipped and slid her way around to the driver's side and pounded on the glass. No response. As Kristin opened the door, the man slumped further forward against his steering wheel. The Lexus horn blasted. It was not an elegant sound. It was a bleating-goat-in-heat sound. Not what she would've expected from the LS.

Kristin pushed the man back against the seat. "Mister, if you're dead, I'll kill you!" she yelled at the top of her lungs.

A thread of drool hung from his lower lip and pooled in the man's jowls.

Older guys, thought Kristin. Yuck.

Kenneth:

Kenneth floated in and out of consciousness.

[78]

It sounded like there was a woodpecker pecking at the window of the car.

Then all was silent and empty.

He thought he heard Lorraine yelling at him.

Blackness, again.

Kenneth opened his eyes and saw a woman coming around the front of the car towards his door. Had he called another hooker? When? He wasn't that out of it, was he? He hadn't done two in a day for at least ten years. Besides, this one looked a bit long in the tooth, for him anyway.

Poof. Back to nothingness. No nice white lights, long airy tunnels. No pearly gates. No one to greet him. Just fuzz. Static.

He heard Lorraine again. What was she saying? She'd kill him? Screw it. Kenneth wouldn't blame her if she did. He was already dying, and if anyone deserved to deliver the final blow, it was Lorraine. Sure, she'd be sad for a while, but she'd be better off without him. She'd probably end up with that little weasel Joe Piscatoris from across the street. Fucker had always wanted to get in her pants.

"Don't, Lorraine," Kenneth cried out. Or thought he cried out. "Joe's a perv. Worse than me."

Then the sensation of being shoved back against his seat. Kenneth hoped whatever came next felt a little nicer.

Kyle and Kristin:

No one else could maneuver this well, thought Kyle. Snow drifts and ice patches. He figured he'd make a really good stunt driver. That'd be a better route than stand-up comedy, even. Or maybe he could do both.

But there was someone else driving around. Not driving, but, like, around. The lucky dog in the Escalade who had almost rear-ended him. The car was sitting in the far left HOV lane as if it were the drive-thru at McDonald's. Kyle peered through his side window as he passed, trying to get a glimpse of the driver, but all he could see were two little kids pressing their faces against the glass in the back seat, waving at him. Clowning around.

Kids always knew how to make the best of a bad situation. Kyle liked little kids. Maybe it was because he had a knack for getting down to their level.

Maybe he should be a teacher. Or a coach. Kyle smiled at the kids and raised his left hand in a finger-tinkling wave as he drove by.

Kyle turned forward just as the woman appeared in front of his car waving her arms like an E-high teenybopper at a rave. He slammed on the Cutlass' pathetic brakes and cranked the wheel to the right, narrowly missing her as she screamed bloody murder. The Cutlass went into a spin, finally coming to a dead halt a few yards forward.

"Fucking crazy bitch!" Kyle yelled. His heart was pounding. Sweat trickled down the back of his neck, mixing with the snowy dampness. Kyle got out of the car and trudged through the snow back towards the woman. He was about to give her hell, but found her slumped over like a sack of dirty clothes that would never, ever make their way to the laundromat.

Oh my fucking god, he thought, I killed her. Then the woman's head popped up like a jack-in-the-box, her face bright red, her eyes giant brown darts.

"You jerk! You've destroyed my Loubotin!" Kristin looked up at the loser who had nipped her foot. He was barely adult, with a scraggly beard and dirty, wet hair hanging past his chin. Another boy, like Craig. Her life seemed to be at the mercy of half-men.

"Destroyed who?" Kyle checked the area surrounding the raving woman, looking for another body.

Kristin lifted her foot and winced.

Kyle could make out the shape of a high heel dangling off the end of a shoe. The snow was pounding down on Kyle's head, and his precious jacket was getting wrecked. He wanted to go back to Brian's crap-car and keep driving. Leave this nasty crazy bitch. But he couldn't.

"And my foot is probably broken," she groaned.

"Sorry," Kyle shrugged, thinking, you shouldn't have run out in front of my car, you psycho asshole.

"You have to help me."

[81]

"Yeah, sure."

"You have to help me move him."

"Who? Lou Button?" Kyle looked around again. There was definitely no one else there. This chick was really tripping out. Walking around on the LIE in a snowstorm. Yelling about some guy named Lou. In high heels, no less. Yeah. Crazy. A stark-raving mad lunatic.

What a total ignoramus, thought Kristin. But keep calm, you need him. "No," she grunted. "Not my shoe. Him." She pointed ahead. "In the Lexus. I think he had a heart attack."

Kyle looked to where Kristin pointed. He saw tail lights and heard the unmistakable purring idle of a luxury vehicle.

Kristin put her foot down and winced. "Ow. Fuck."

"I said I was sorry," Kyle hugged himself, defensive and freezing.

"What. Ever." Kristin grunted.

"So, where do you want me to move the guy?"

"Back to my car." She glanced back towards the Escalade.

Aha! It figured. He imagined her living in one of those faux-farmhouses they put up in the old potato fields in Brookdale. He was willing to bet she was crazy and rich.

"I'll call for an ambulance," Kristin continued, thinking out loud. "I'll be crying. If they know I'm with someone old, a sick senior, they'll come to me quicker. And I'll insist they take me and the kids as well. I'll say we're his family."

"Are you?" asked Kyle.

Kristin looked up at Kyle as if seeing him for the first time. "Am I what?"

"Family." Kyle noticed that, with her face less flushed and her eyes less wild, the woman looked like an older version of Brittany DeMarco. A pouty, snooty Brittany, ten years from now.

Kristin rolled her eyes. "Yeah, sure. Whatever. We're family."

Kyle started to trudge towards the Lexus.

"Wait, you idiot!" yelled Kristin. "Carry me back to my car first. I'm not exactly loving this sitting on a highway in a frigging blizzard thing, thank you very much."

The woman raised her arms to Kyle. It seemed weird because of the Brittany similarity, a turn off and a turn on at the same time. Kyle let her clasp her hands around his neck. He hoisted her up, then shifted his arms under her butt, to the crook of her knees. She panted against the side of his neck, in hard short puffs. Her breath was warm. And she wasn't all that heavy. This part of things was kind of nice. Kyle managed to get her back to her fancy car, deposited her by the driver's side door. The bitch didn't even thank him. Any thrill was totally gone.

[83]

Jordan and Larissa had clambered all over Kristin's beloved tan leather seats in their dirty snow boots. Gummy bears had been smushed in to the side windows like colored bird turds.

"Cute kids," Kyle chuckled.

Kristin glared at the man-boy. "Just go get the old guy and bring him back here before he croaks, okay?"

"Whatever," Kyle grunted. He walked to the Lexus wet and frozen from head to toe. Jacket wrecked. Feet numb. Icicles hanging from his beard. At least, maybe, the sick old geezer would show him some respect.

Kenneth and Kyle:

"Sweet Jesus! You've come to save me!" Kenneth was happy. Deliriously happy.

Kyle smiled. The man's eyes were wild, but he was very much alive. "Hey dude. You alright?"

"I am now, thank God," Kenneth nodded. "Now that you're here, oh Lord."

Talk about respect, thought Kyle. All these church-y words. This is awesome. "Okay. Cool. I'm gonna take you back to that lady's car."

"What lady?"

"The one who found you. She's gonna call an ambulance."

"Mary?"

[84]

"Um, maybe. I don't know her name."

"The Mother of God?" Kenneth grabbed the slippery sleeves of Kyle's leather jacket and stared at him, demented and desperate. "No. No. It's the other Mary. Mary Magdalene. She's the whore, right? Your friend? The girl apostle? It was her. Here, before."

"She's no friend of mine," said Kyle.

"Then it's Lorraine," Kenneth cried. "Please God, tell me it's Lorraine."

The old guy needed to be calmed down. His eyes were googly. Something was off. "Could be," Kyle nodded. "Yeah. Sure it is. It's Lorraine."

"Lorraine," Kenneth moaned. "I'm sorry, Honey. Sorry for everything." He started to lift himself off his seat, but collapsed back, short of breath. There was still pain, though not as intense, radiating from his chest down his left arm.

"Whoa, dude." Kyle patted Kenneth on the shoulder. "Take it easy."

Kenneth nodded, and caught his breath.

Kyle managed to get him out of the car by draping Kenneth's bulky arm around his own narrow shoulders. No way he could carry this guy the way he'd carried Lorraine. Or Mary. Or whatever the snoot-queen's name was. "I've got you, but you'll have to walk with me."

"Whatever you say. Oh Sweet Jesus. Whatever you say."

"Okay, sir. Let's take it real slow." Kyle dragged Kenneth back towards the Escalade. Soon they'd all be together. Maybe the snarky bitch would thank him. He wasn't expecting a full-on make-out session, but a grateful kiss on the cheek would be nice. Maybe the kids would share their snacks. Kyle was kinda munched out. Meanwhile, the old guy was smiling up at him like he was some kind of savior. Kyle felt important. Actually, dare he think it, he felt holy. Which got Kyle thinking: Maybe this is it? Maybe this is my calling?

A Melody

Barney J. Mackenzie stopped singing when the phone rang. He snapped off the transistor radio midway through "Moonlight in Vermont," cleared his throat, and picked up the receiver.

"Casa Tortuga Security. This is Barney." His voice reverb-rumbled deep inside his gut. Maybe he was getting the hang of this security business after all.

"This is Pauline Berger, Mrs. Berger's daughter?"

Mrs. Berger was a tiny old gal, close to ninety years old, who walked the manicured paths of Casa Tortuga daily, spindly and lopsided, skittering like a cricket with a bum leg. She was one of the few residents Barney had met face-to-face in his two weeks working security at Casa Tortuga Condominiums. Mrs. Berger was still full of beans, thought Barney. Full of beans.

"What can I do for you, Pauline?" he asked.

"I've been trying to reach my mother for over two hours, and I keep getting a busy signal. I'm sure it's just that the phone is off the hook, or that damn Melody wreaking havoc again. But God forbid there's a real problem. Mama's pretty with it, but lately she's had some,

[87]

um, moments. Would you mind going over to the apartment and checking for me?"

"No problem. We'll send someone over there right away. Which building is your mother in?"

"She's in the Mimosa. Number 306."

"Okey-dokey." Barney scribbled down the info in the security log. "And what's the best contact number to call you back at?"

"212-858-1107."

A New York area code. Barney liked New Yorkers. They were a minority at Casa Tortuga, as most Gulf Coast seasonal residents were Midwestern retirees. Barney didn't have anything against Midwesterners, but when he'd owned his store, Kiddles Toy Shoppe, he'd found them a bit hard to read. They were smiley for sure, but they never told him what they really wanted. New Yorkers, on the other hand, did so right from the get go.

"Okay Pauline. 212-858-1107. I'll get back to you pronto."

Just as Barney picked up his walkie-talkie to radio Gunther, the guard on foot patrol (FP, in guard lingo), the latter knocked on the entrance booth window.

"Yo, old man," Gunther drawled in thick Bayou slobber, "Git your sorry ass outta that booth. You're on foot, I'm on booth. I'm gonna sit on that chair there and have me some lunch."

Gunther always got booth duty at the hottest time of day, while Barney was making the rounds in the sweltering sun. Gunther had worked at Casa Tortuga for ten years, straight out of high school. "A tub of lard, with a strychnine streak and a pickled brain," was how the supervisor described Gunther to Barney on his first day. At the time it seemed cruel. Lately, not so.

"Come on then, git." Gunther opened the EB door and shooed Barney along.

If this were Kiddles Toy Shoppe, Barney would've taken Gunther by his chubby earlobe and dragged him out the door and on to the sidewalk. But Barney had no clout at Casa Tortuga, no seniority over Gunther, even with forty years on the fool. Barney hadn't a speck of authority, but for issuing the occasional reminder to someone's grandchild not to run on the pool deck or stick their bubble gum under the plastic webbing of the chaise lounges.

Barney edged past Gunther's yeasty fermented stench. "A call came in from a family member to check on a resident."

"Whatever," Gunther sighed. He slapped open the log book and scribbled a hasty note. The springs of his chair screeched like a pack of dying muskrats. "Which old sack of bones is it?"

"Mrs. Berger in Mimosa 306."

Gunther sat forward, the chair springs wailing a reverse arpeggio. "Aw shit. I should take this one."

Did Gunther think Barney incapable of a simple house visit? At least with this, Barney could keep the young idiot in his place. "No. No." Barney thrust his hand out in a traffic-cop-worthy pose. "It's on my watch. You just keep sitting there and let that fan do its thing."

Barney could hear Gunther grumbling obscenities at his back as he headed down the crushed seashell path towards Mimosa 306.

+ + + + + + +

Barney pressed the button in the center of the starfish-shaped doorbell. He was a tad surprised when a young woman answered. Mrs. Berger was an 'Independent'—Casa Tortuga Security lingo for elderly residents living on their own. As far as Barney knew, Mrs. Berger did not have a nurse, or home aid.

"Hey," said the woman. "What's up?"

Barney guessed she was somewhere in her late 20's, though he was no expert when it came to guessing ages, especially of anyone under 60. There were no wrinkles on her tanned and freckled face, and she had what his wife Greta would call 'Breck Girl Hair,' meaning it was dark brown, thick, and so long it almost looked fake. Another man might find her sexy, but Barney wasn't one to go for girls this young or this skinny.

"I'm Barney from Security."

"Hi Barney from Security. What's up?"

Barney heard a bird chirping inside the apartment and Mrs. Berger singing "Night and day, you are the one..." behind the partially-closed front door.

"Pardon me, but is Mrs. Berger in?" He tried for that belly-rumbling deepness he'd mastered when answering the front booth phone, but what came out was monotone and flat.

"I'm sorry. She's kinda busy right now." The young woman wore blue cutoff jean shorts and a flimsy top that looked like a handkerchief tied together behind her neck and waist. She was holding a light blue envelope with a handwritten address on it. You didn't see too many of those these days, thought Barney. It was all bills, or junk mail. No one wrote letters, at least not to him. The young woman leaned forward, and in a tobacco-infused whisper she said: "Grandma's using the toilet."

"I didn't know Mrs. Berger had a granddaughter," Barney said. Then a lightbulb went off in his head. "Ah! Pauline just mentioned you on the phone. You must be Melody."

Her face scrunched up prune-like for a split second, then she smiled. Her teeth were perfectly straight, but dishwater dull. "That's right. I'm Grandma's best kept secret," she declared, emphasizing 'Grandma' like a special at the local supermarket.

So the havoc-wreaking Melody was family, thought Barney. Mrs. Berger was a chatterbox, would talk his ear off if he ran into her during FP rounds. She'd even visited him a few times in the EB where they bonded over their mutual love of show tunes. Mrs. Berger bragged about Pauline, the lawyer daughter in Manhattan, and

David, the doctor son in Denver. She hadn't mentioned any grandchildren. But then again, neither had Barney, and he had one grandchild of his own.

"Welcome to Casa Tortuga, Melody. When did you arrive?"

"Late last night. Like, maybe two in the morning?" She glanced down at the envelope in her hand and shoved it in her back pocket. "My flight from Denver was wicked delayed." She scratched her bare, exceptionally thin arm. Barney noted a few red marks. Bug bites, probably, he thought. The mosquitoes were relentless this time of year.

"Oh, so you must be David's daughter."

Melody's blue eyes sparkled like a fake sapphire ring from a gum ball machine. "Yeah. David. That's right."

"My son lives in Denver also," Barney blurted. He hadn't confessed this coincidence to Mrs. Berger, what with her David a successful oncologist and his son Brian a new agey self-seeker. But something about Melody's twinkling eyes made Barney reveal this kismet-y connection. "Maybe you know him. Brian Mackenzie?"

She shook her head. "Sorry. Nope."

"He runs the Arcadian Dream Wellness Spa with his wife Jalilah. They have a daughter. Calliope."

Melody shrugged. "It's kind of a big city."

"Of course it is." Barney had only visited Denver once, on his own, eleven years earlier, after Calliope had been born, home-birthed in a bathtub, in Brian and Jalilah's cramped and dingy apartment. His wife hadn't gone with him, wouldn't ever go. Greta swore off contact with Brian after he'd left Long Boat with Jalilah, who was as tall, dark, and exotic as Brian was short, pale, and average. "Anyhow Melody, it seems there's a problem with the phone. Your aunt's been trying to reach here for over an hour. Could you check and see if any of the landlines are off the hook?"

"Um sure. No problem," Melody said. "Thanks for telling me. Bye."

She was about to close the door when Barney said, "I'm sorry, but I'm required to stay until I know everything is okay."

"That's really not necessary," Melody said.

Barney nodded. "I know. But rules are rules."

She sighed. "Okay. Wait right here. I'll be back in a sec."

Melody walked back inside, leaving the door slightly ajar. Casa Tortuga Security Rule Number Four: Never enter a resident's apartment unless invited in, or in case of emergency. But that didn't stop Barney from furtively poking his head in for a quick peek.

Mrs. Berger's apartment was neat and clean, but stunk of tobacco. A large battered rolling suitcase was propped by a coat rack shaped like a palm tree. A bright pink and bangly sweater hung from one of the fronds. There was a pack of Marlboro Lights on the driftwood hallway table. Next to the cigarettes was a set of keys on a "Phantom of the Opera" keychain. The cigarettes were most likely Melody's, and might account for her less than perfect teeth, but the key chain had to belong to the mistress of the house; that tiny, tune crazy soprano, Mrs. Berger.

Grandmother and granddaughter were in the master bedroom, behind a closed door. Their voices were muffled, but the bird's chirping was sharp and familiar. Pure parakeet. Barney knew this tweeting tune because he had a parakeet of his own. His Sammy had reigned from a large cage set next to the Kiddles cash register, singing while Greta tallied up sales. No question the bird had been good for business, especially since Greta wasn't keen on small talk.

Once Kiddles went down the tubes and the foreclosure was a done deal, Barney took Sammy home. He set his cage up by the kitchen window, hoping Sammy might enjoy the view, no longer having customer contact for stimulation. But Sammy barely sang these days. A feeble twitter when hungry, maybe. Not much else.

Mrs. Berger's bedroom door opened, and Barney caught a glimpse of the old girl sitting on the edge of her bed, hands resting in her lap, chin lifted and smile joyous like a Born Again on Easter Sunday. All seemed well in Mimosa 306. Yes, indeed.

Barney pulled his head back into the vestibule when Melody left the bedroom. He looked down at his clipboard, pretending to read as she approached.

"You were right," Melody said. "The phone in the bedroom was off the hook. She lets that bird out of the cage and it flies all over the place knocking stuff over."

Barney also let Sammy fly free when Greta wasn't home. "It's a parakeet, right?"

Melody shrugged. "Um, I think so. I don't really know that much about birds."

"It's good for them to spread their wings a bit."

"Yeah, right," Melody smiled. If she were Barney's granddaughter he'd say a thing or two about the smoking and those teeth. "Escape from their little birdy prisons."

Barney looked down. "Something like that, I suppose."

"I'll make sure Grandma calls my aunt and tells her everything's fine. Thanks, Barney. So cool you came here to check on things."

Barney shrugged. "Just part of my job."

+++++++

Trying to hold on to Kiddles had wiped Barney out financially. His bankruptcy was a shameful fact Greta reminded him of almost every evening. But that night her contempt was directed at her new place of employment.

"What a bunch of idiots," Greta grumbled as she tugged her official Walmart polo shirt over her head. She hunched on the closed toilet seat, her thin grey hair a halo of fluff around her skull, barely there, almost beside the point. The weight of her breasts pulled the straps of her brassiere so the cups stretched like swinging baskets off her knobby shoulders.

"Idiot customers or idiot employees?" Barney asked.

Greta looked up at him, her dry lips a downward crescent. "Does it really make a difference?"

"Just trying to make polite conversation," he shrugged.

"Always the gentleman," Greta muttered as she bent to unlace ugly, black, built for comfort shoes. "Everyone's Gentle Giant."

Barney was six four in stocking feet, with a bit of a gut. His size was the only reason he'd gotten the Casa Tortuga job. People liked their security guards on the big side. But Barney was no ruthless foil to robbers, rapists, con artist, or thieves. He could no more throw a punch than he could fly a spaceship.

"I'm on Entrance Booth duty tonight," he nearly winced while delivering the news. "Gotta be back there at eight."

Greta stood. She was tiny, like Mrs. Berger, but with none of the spritely energy the older woman had in spades. "I suppose you'll want some dinner then."

Greta shuffled away and grabbed her faded housedress from its designated hook. At Kiddles she had always made a point to dress in a nice bright outfit to match the mood of the store. Greta knew it was good for business to mask her own sourpuss nature while Barney worked the floor. He was the jovial presence, chatting with customers, laughing at jokes, rewinding wind-up toys that skittered and barked and flipped on the store's checkerboard floor.

Barney and Greta watched the evening news while eating chicken cutlets, instant mashed potatoes, and microwaved green beans. A four-car collision near the airport, a cut in funding for state-run daycare, spring training for the major leagues underway.

"I met a nice young girl from Denver today," Barney said, once the news was off and he'd started stacking plates.

Greta stared at Sammy, watching as the bird pecked at his water tube.

Barney filled the sink to pre-rinse the dishes. When Brian was a boy living at home, one of his chores was to load the dishwasher according to Greta's specifications; big plates in the back, salad plates in the front, knifes blade down, forks tongs up. All glassware on the top rack. When he hit the teen years, Brian always loaded at least one knife upright, a sharp head raised in silver, silent protest.

"She's staying with her grandmother," Barney continued, pretending it was a conversation. "That woman I told you about. Mrs. Berger."

"The show tune lady," Greta said. "The one who actually talks to the security guards."

"Yes."

[97]

"And?"

"I asked her if she knew Brian and Jalilah." He scraped an inconsequential dollop of mashed potato in to the garbage pail.

Greta rose from the table. "I think the bird needs more water."

+++++++

Barney arranged his thermos of milky tea, trusty transistor radio, and a mystery paperback he probably wouldn't read on the EB countertop. Before he tuned in to WBBX, he decided to make a quick call.

"Hello?" Pauline Berger answered.

"Hi Pauline, this is Barney from Casa Tortuga Condominiums calling."

"Oh dear. Is there another problem?"

"No, not at all," Barney could've kicked himself for not getting to the point immediately. It was in the handbook, after all. State your purpose immediately so residents and guests are not caused any undue distress. "I just wanted to make sure you spoke with your mother this afternoon."

"Oh," he could hear her relax. "Yes. I spoke with her. She sounded fine. I guess it was that bird again."

"Seems so," Barney paused, then added, "It's nice that Melody is there with her."

Pauline laughed. "Maybe. But what a nuisance sometimes."

Sure, young people could be annoying, but wasn't it precious to have grandchildren? Grandchildren who came to visit? And children who called you in Florida to check that everything was okay? To mention these sentiments to a resident's daughter seemed against regulations. Or maybe just Barney's personal ones. "Have a nice evening Pauline," he said, trying again for that authoritative basso, "And please let us know if there's anything else we can do."

The night passed in a slow humid thrum. Barney was coated in Floridian sweat shellac, even with the fan set high. WBBX was doing a Sondheim special, not one of Barney' favorite composers, too hard to sing along to. Still he tried, stumbling a beat behind most selections until "Send in the Clowns," which he managed to finish with a modicum of vocal pride.

He swiveled in his chair and surveyed the buildings of Casa Tortuga, settling his gaze on the Mimosa. He imagined Melody and Mrs. Berger up there in 306, cuddled on an overstuffed sofa, maybe watching a comedy on TV. He wondered if Calliope ever watched TV, or if Brian and Jalilah even owned one.

Barney swiveled back in the direction of the front gate. That was his job. That should be his focus. He turned the music up. "Another Hundred People," from Company. Impossible to sing. He sipped some tea and tried to read.

+++++++

Barney's shift ended at 2 a.m. He got home a half hour later. He'd be bunking down in Brian's old room because Greta hated to be disturbed once her bedside reading light was off.

Brian's room was filled with boxes of old Kiddles inventory that hadn't been liquidated. Outdated Barbies and Pogo Sticks. Magic Sets and Monopoly. An entire set of no-longer-collectable Beanie Babies. Barney planned to sell the stuff on eBay, if he could ever figure out how to set up an account.

His son's old twin bed was shoved in the corner, the navy blue bedspread printed all over with tiny white whales, no two facing the same way. It was the sort of random design that kept a young Brian occupied for hours as he tried to discover a clue, a pattern, a reason. But Barney was an old man with weakening eyes who'd had a long, perplexing night. If he stared too long at the white whales he might get dizzy, so he averted his eyes, stripped to his shorts, got in the narrow bed and pulled the covers up.

Sleep was slow to come.

+++++++

Barney returned to Casa Tortuga at 2 p.m., ready for FP, sunglasses on, his balding pate coated with SPF 50, as headgear of any kind was not allowed, according to the handbook. He walked the required routes like a rat in a maze. At around 5 p.m. as the sun was starting to settle down, he saw Melody and Mrs. Berger sitting on a bench by the man-made pond between the Mimosa and the Sargasso. Mrs. Berger stared at the bubbling fountain in the center of the pond, clapping each time the plumes of water rose in a predictable pulse. Melody scratched and fidgeted, sneaking glances up at the Mimosa over the top of Mrs. Berger's tiny, sun-bonneted head.

When Melody saw Barney she froze, a look of panic blooming on her face, as if Barney were a crocodile about to slither over and gobble her up. Barney felt her alarm like a punch in the solar plexus. Was she truly scared of Barney? Then he reasoned: maybe it wasn't him at all. Maybe something else had unnerved Melody long before he'd arrived. Yes, he thought, something else is terribly wrong. He needed to go over and see if he could be of service.

As he approached, Melody grabbed Mrs. Berger by the arm and hoisted her up off the bench.

"Ouch," Mrs. Berger snapped.

"Sorry Honey," Melody said. "Time to get back upstairs."

"Everything okay here, ladies?" Barney asked.

"Everything's great." Melody shot Barney a high beam smile. Then holding Mrs. Berger at a distance she leaned towards him and whispered: "Just need to get Grandma upstairs for her nap."

Barney glanced over at Mrs. Berger, who looked mighty chipper underneath the floppy brim of her bonnet.

"Everything alright, Mrs. Berger?" Barney said loudly.

"Rosy, Dollface. Just rosy," Mrs. Berger nodded.

"Okay then," Barney said, feeling there was more to say, but not knowing what it was that needed the saying.

"Come on Grandma." Melody's voice was a cool ooze with gravely undertones. All those cigarettes, thought Barney. She'll be sounding like a trucker by the time she's thirty.

Mrs. Berger tripped down the path holding hands with Melody. Barney was about to follow them when the old lady began belting "Everything's Coming Up Roses" with Merman-esque gusto. Any self-respecting musical theater buff knew this meant things were pretty peachy. Barney let the pair walk away from him, let them enjoy their bond.

They disappeared behind a giant oleander bush. Barney, no longer feeling quite so purposeful, decided to change course. Required routes be damned. He turned in the opposite direction and made a long loop around the Casa Tortuga perimeter. He walked along the beachfront and watched turquoise Gulf wavelets lap anemically onto powdery white sand. He collected stray bits of litter from around rubbish bins with fake giant tortoiseshell tops that consistently malfunctioned, keeping only the heaviest trash contained. He passed the Palm Tree Putting Range, where men his own age with too much time on their hands pushed little white balls into holes over and over and over. He tried hard not to be awash with envy.

+++++++

Greta had put some effort into dinner, which was unexpected, given their current circumstances. There was a salad with crisper-than-usual lettuce, and some nice nuggety tomatoes, and grilled local mahi-mahi.

Barney forced himself to eat heartily, though he was feeling down in the dumps. Even on the drive home, with "Some Enchanted Evening" blasting on WBBX, he'd been unable to shake his memory of Melody's horrified look when he'd approached her earlier that day.

Then, as if she were the mind reader Barney sometimes feared she was, Greta asked, "Any chit-chatting today with your young Denver friend?"

Barney took a deliberately large bite of fish, buying time. If Greta had been a different kind of wife, he might have told her about the odd happenings by the pond. He might have gotten some support, some 'for better or worse' sort of stuff. But he was never quite sure when or how Greta's fickle moods and judgements would show themselves.

"Nope. Not a word," he finally said.

"Colorado," Greta shook her head. "I still don't get why anyone would want to live in the middle of the country so far from the ocean."

[103]

"You're talking about Brian," Barney sighed. "So far from us, you mean."

"I wasn't talking about Brian," Greta's voice was a husky desert. "I was talking about that girl. Besides, Brian made his choice a long time ago."

Thirteen years ago this August, thought Barney.

Greta stabbed a blue cheese dressed lettuce leaf and stuffed it in her mouth, her lips milky as she chomped like a dull cow. Had there actually been something attractive about Greta's solemnity back when they were young? Barney could barely remember. They'd met working their way through community college, Barney stocking shelves at a Tampa Winn-Dixie, Greta the quiet but petite and pretty cashier at checkout number four. Even back then, he recalled, she'd never been one to savor or stockpile joy.

"Calliope turns twelve next month," Barney said breezily, as if noting a slight change in air temperature.

Greta stabbed more lettuce.

"I'm thinking of going to Denver for her birthday."

"And how exactly do you plan to get there?" Greta asked. "We don't have any money for airplanes. Besides, I strongly doubt the powers-that-be at Casa Tortuga are going to let you take vacation time when you've only been working there for a month."

"I said I was thinking of going. I didn't say I was going."

"Well don't go making any mistakes. We can't afford for you to do something dumb and lose that job."

"I would just like to see my granddaughter, that's all. It's not right for all this time to go by."

"It's a two way street, Barney. They could get off their airy fairy behinds and come here. Bring her to visit us." Greta glugged her ginger ale till the last ice cube knocked her teeth. She set the tumbler down on the table like a gavel. "Meanwhile, just send her another card."

+++++++

The next morning Gunther called in sick. The supervisor told Barney he thought it was bullshit, that Gunther "finally got himself a piece of ass and was holding on to it for dear life." Whatever the reason, a guy named Roland filled in, which was okay with Barney because Roland and he tag-teamed in a copacetic fashion, trading EB and FP duties on an hourly basis, which made for shorter walking stints, less boredom, tired feet, and sun exposure. Barney was on his second FP round when Roland radioed. Pauline Berger called. It seemed her mother's phone was off the hook again.

Barney wasn't thrilled about a return visit to Mimosa 306. He was starting to agree with Pauline. Melody was a nuisance. The thought of dealing with her stuck in his craw. Her herky jerky manner with her grandmother. Her saccharine smile. Her bad teeth. Her scurrying away from him as if he had a highly contagious disease. But security was Barney's duty, and a job was a job.

He walked by a planting of succulents, odd twisted green monsters with spikes, blobby appendages, and little hairs that begged to be shaved. He thought, what kind of granddaughter doesn't even notice when a bird knocks the phone off the hook? Probably busy talking to her friends on her cell phone. Or texting. That's what young people do now more than anything. They text. They don't even know how to have a nice, honest, face-to-face conversation. For all he knew Calliope was just the same. Just the same.

Once inside the lobby of the Mimosa, he decided to forgo the elevator and get to 306 via the underused stairway. After all, he was fit as a fiddle, no old codger, not someone to be dismissed.

Barney wasn't sure if the queasy feeling in his gut was the result of taking the stairs at an over-ambitious clip or because Mrs. Berger's front door was wide, wide open. The skunky smell coming from within the apartment activated a sense memory: fifteen-year-old Brian sprawled on his whale-covered bedspread smoking a joint and staring with teenage indifference at Barney, who had barged in at Greta's behest.

"Hello, Mrs. Berger? Melody?" Barney called through the entry to 306.

No answer, just humming and bird song. An open door and lack of response combined were categorized in the handbook as an emergency. Therefore, Barney walked into the apartment through a smoky haze. The suitcase was gone, as were the pink sweater, the cigarettes, and Mrs. Berger's keys. The rest of the apartment was in shambles. Clothes were scattered everywhere, tropical print casualties with sleeves and pant legs askew. Orthopedic shoes, dangerously tossed on the plush white carpet, jutted like rocks. Every drawer in every kitchen cabinet splayed open. A couch with no seat cushions pulled to the middle of the ransacked living room. The missing cushions outside on the sun deck with cottony innards spewing out of large gashes in the canvas fabric. A kitchen knife gleaming in sunlight on the stucco floor.

Barney found Mrs. Berger sitting on her bed next to an empty fire-proof valuables box, humming a gobblety gook of familiar riffs. As soon as Barney recognized a tune, Mrs. Berger changed it to something nonsensical, atonal, and out of touch.

The parakeet flew around the room, chirping nervously, unsure what to do with itself. It attempted to land on a pile of clothing, expecting solid ground perhaps, but fluttered away when its talons touched the soft velour of a disheveled dressing gown.

"Jesus Christ," Barney yelped. "Mrs. Berger. What happened?"

She looked up at him and it was obvious. Mrs. Berger was stoned out of her gourd. Her eyes were unfocused but not unnerved. Again Barney was reminded of teenage Brian.

The old lady held a lit joint and was about to burn a hole in her lotus-blossomed duvet. Barney wrenched the joint out of Mrs. Berger's hand and crushed it, searing his palm like a stigmata. "Where did you get this?" he cried.

"Skinny Minny, of course. I'm so glad that Chubby Wubby introduced us." Mrs. Berger rubbed her small globe of a belly. "She made marvelous pancakes this morning. That fat security guard, though." She shook her head like a pre-school teacher shaming a student who had swiped the red crayon. "He made quite the mess."

"Gunther?" cried Barney.

Mrs. Berger nodded.

"Casa Tortuga Gunther?"

"That's right, Gunther," she frowned. "He took my parasol. The one I used in the Community Center revival of Carousel in 1989."

"Where's your granddaughter?"

"Don't be ridiculous," Mrs. Berger giggled. "I don't have any grandchildren."

Of course, no grandchildren, thought Barney. She would've mentioned them the first time you met her. Every old person boasts about grandchildren if they have them. Except for you, you absurd and clueless man.

The light blue envelope Melody-the-non-grandchild had stuck in her back pocket when Barney first met her was now on the bedroom floor. Barney picked it up. It was addressed to Mrs. Berger, and the return address was from David Berger, 109 Mountain View Drive, Denver, Colorado. The handwriting was clear, legible. It had been easy for Melody to read in a sidewise glance. Easy to fabricate a familial connection. She'd done this expertly while being questioned by an incompetent fool named Barney.

"Where's Melody?"

Mrs. Berger sighed. "Here, of course." She lifted her arm, over-tanned and age spotted flesh sagging on a near skeletal frame. The parakeet landed at the crook of her wrist and Mrs. Berger lifted her pet to her face. The bird gave the old lady a gentle peck on the lips. "My little Melody. Right where she belongs."

Barney moaned, imagining Gunther and the skinny, scabby woman careening down the highway in Mrs. Berger's barely-used Subaru, bound for Lord-knows-where. He imagined precious pieces of Mrs. Berger's life shoved carelessly in that horrid rolling suitcase, or tossed like trash in the back of the car. Gunther, that tub of lard with a strychnine streak and Whatever-Her-Name-Was, his piece of ass with rotting teeth, were long gone by now. Long gone.

Melody alit from Mrs. Berger's wrist, spreading pitch-perfect agitation and bird poop. But Mrs. Berger looked happier than the day Barney first met her, when she'd stood outside the EB and delivered a soulful rendition of "As Long as He Needs Me." Back when

Barney's job at Casa Tortuga seemed like a fresh start, not the dead end it had just become.

Blossoms

On the sweltering camp bus, girls leaned against each other, holding hands, whispering, an epidemic of Siamese twins. It was August 17, 1969, Ellie's eleventh birthday and she'd woken to the news that she would be going on a cruddy hike led by Harold, the Nature counselor. All the girls from the Daisy, Rose, and Tulip Bunks were there, but the only seat left was next to Debby, aka Bug Eye, who was another Daisy, and the only camper more outside things than Ellie herself. Debby smelled like tropical BO because she rarely showered, gooping herself all over with Coconut Skin Trip instead. Debby was funny, sometimes, but mostly she was a klutz who made babyish jokes. Plus, she had that one eye, the Bug Eye, which seemed to wander off on its own accord.

Ellie felt like the real Nowhere Man at Camp Lakawalla. The other girls in Ellie's bunk were Full Session, and had been there since the beginning of July. Ellie was an August Session Only. By the time she'd arrived, friendships were firmly knotted, and she was a loose, unnecessary thread. She'd been hoping her birthday would tie her in. She'd seen other kids with summer birthdays sauntering down the dirt paths from Arts and

Crafts with paper birthday crowns covered in pompoms, ribbons, and Mylar streamers, an entourage of bunkmates nipping at their heels. At lunch, there was always a cake with frosting and candles, and everyone screaming the Happy Birthday song. They got to do their favorite Lakawalla Activity any time during the day, even if their bunk wasn't scheduled to do so. Ellie was going to pick Waterfront. But what did Ellie get instead? A walk in the buggy woods, a soggy sandwich and a shallow stream. Big whoop, she thought. Happy Birthday to me.

Harold stood from his seat behind the bus driver and turned to face the busload of girls. "Blossoms." He nodded his head a little up and forward like he was grooving to an inner beat. "We're going deep in the woods, where Nature rules." Harold said Nature like a horse braying. Nayychure.

Harold was ancient. Not quite as old as Ellie's parents, but close. He was a real deal hippy, not like the suburban teenage hippies back in Great Neck. Those younger guys wore caftans and huaraches and had straggly long hair and beards like Harold. They made peace signs with their fingers in greeting and played flutes and guitars. But they still lived in nice houses with lawns. Their VWs were serviced by the same mechanics as their parents' BMWs. Ellie's seventeen-year-old sister Hannah went steady with one of them. His name was Arthur, but he wanted to be called Arlo, like Arlo Guthrie. Everyone called him Arlo, except his parents.

Hannah thought Arlo was "far out." Ellie thought far out was a dopey place for a boyfriend to be.

"I want everyone to respect the forest. No littering. No plucking pretty blossoms, Blossoms," Harold paused for laughs at his flower joke. None of the campers laughed. So Harold switched gears, pressing his palms together in front of his chest and solemnly adding, "We'll leave everything as it is. In perfect harmony." He bowed his head, and Ellie could see pink scalp through thinning hair. When Harold sat down, almost every Blossom stuck their thumbs in their ears and wiggled their fingers at his oblivious back. Not Ellie. She just turned to look out the window at the boring scenery. Trees, trees, and more trees.

"Surry down to a stone soul picnic..." A voice sang from the back of the bus, the sacred Tulips Only Section, where the oldest Blossoms, ages 14-15, sat away from the younger girls. The singer was Joy Kramer, a girl from Great Neck whom Ellie knew because Joy was sort of, but not really, friends with Ellie's sister Iris. Even though she was only fifteen, Joy was built like a big galumphy woman. She had a real bosom, a shelf made out of breasts. Some of the other Tulips had bosoms, too, but Joy's was definitely the most va-va-va-voom.

"There will be lots of time and wine..." Joy continued on her own for one more line, belting in a deep voice that sounded like it belonged to a forty-year-old. Other than her big chest, Joy didn't have much going for

[113]

her in the looks department. Her eyes were tiny slits, like piggy eyes. Her black hair always looked greasy, and clumped around her pimply face like wet seaweed. She had this weird button nose that stuck up so you could see her nostrils, which Ellie thought was gross and made her wonder what Joy did when she had boogers she couldn't hide.

Other Tulips joined in, "Red yellow honey, sassafras and Moonshine..." Ellie found the Tulips annoying. They were always crying, singing, or hugging, all superior and hoity-toity. They wrote in paisley-covered journals with quill pens. Some wore mascara. They used antiperspirant.

"...And from the sky come the Lord and the lightening..." Joy on her own again. Joy did theater back in Great Neck. She got lead parts. In Great Neck, theater kids were sort of losers, not popular at all. In fact, Joy was almost a Debby back home. But at Camp Lakawalla Joy was cool. Go figure.

Joy and the Tulips moved off Laura Nyro and on to the Beatles, singing "Dear Prudence," sticking their own names in, pretending that they were the ones being asked out to play on a lovely day. Ellie closed her eyes and tried to sleep. Eventually her mouth opened and a trickle of drool rivuleted towards her chin, but she didn't have the energy to wipe it away. When the bus came to an abrupt stop, Ellie's head nearly snapped off.

Harold stood from his seat up front and announced: "Blossoms, we've arrived in Heaven. We've got three hours to explore the ridge, eat some grub, and hike our way back down. So let's get truckin.'"

Daisies, Roses, and Tulips spilled out of the bus. With them spilled whines and complaints, because standing out in the sun felt like being covered in hot, wet towels.

"This is retarded," grunted Beth Edelson, a girl from Ellie's bunk who called everyone and everything 'retarded.'

Other girls fanned themselves dramatically, and grumbled like a bunch of losers at the OTB.

Harold ignored all of them. "This way, Blossoms!" He led the way up a trail, stomping in his flimsy huaraches, his hairy calves and calloused heels defying Myrna, the Camp Director, who had given the explicit order for high socks and sturdy shoes.

The woods were moist and cool. No one was in danger of fainting from heat stroke. The girls walked single file down the narrow trail under a canopy of ancient giant trees. No buddy-buddy walking or someone would end up traipsing through poison oak. There were grumbles about snakes or spiders. But mostly they couldn't talk to each other, which sucked because what was the point of anything when you're a girl between the ages of 12-15 and you can't talk?

[115]

"When I find myself in times of trouble, Mother Mary comes to me. Speaking words of wisdom, let it be..." Joy started, but no one joined in. The trail was super steep, and it was hard for anyone but her to sing and hike at the same time. She finally shut up, which was a good thing because it really was too show-offy for Joy to be the only one singing when no one else could, even if she did have the best voice.

For a while the only sounds Ellie heard were boots crunching, birds tweeting, and leaves rustling. No one could talk, no one could be left out, so Ellie was almost enjoying herself, but only almost. She still would've rather been back at camp, throwing herself into the lake like a wild Banshee, gorging on lasagna for lunch, ending with a birthday cake pig-out.

Suddenly, the girls ahead of Ellie stopped walking. Ellie accidentally rammed into the back of Claudia Belsen, a Rose, and not the most understanding of thirteen-year-olds.

"Watch it, Spaz," Claudia snarled.

"Sorry," Ellie muttered.

Up ahead Ellie could see Harold with his pointer finger pressed to his lips, just under his Fu Manchu mustache.

Once everyone was still, Harold said: "Do you hear that music?"

"I hear it," cried Debby.

Did Debby really, Ellie wondered? Or was she just doing what she always did: sucking up and trying too hard?

Within seconds, everyone put in their two cents; I hear it. I don't hear it. You're kidding me, you can't hear that? It's so loud! What are you talking about? Are you deaf? That's just a bunch of birds. No it's a band, cross my heart and hope to die!

Harold pointed towards a different path, one marked with a blue tree disc. "Should we take a detour and investigate?"

Girls shouted "Yeah! Yeah!" Choosing music over Nayychure.

"Harold," a voice called from the back of the line. "We really should do what's planned." It was Ellie's counselor, Lois: a Vassar freshman, and a real stickler for rules. Even when it was raining, Lois made the Daisies do Farm Activity, insisting they slosh through mud mixed with animal poop to pull on goat teats or feed the chickens.

"Come on Lois," Harold smiled, his teeth like a row of yellow corn, "It'll be a gas."

Lois' brow furrowed the way Ellie's mother's brow furrowed when she botched a recipe from her new Julia Child cookbook. Finally Lois relented. "You're the grown-up," she shrugged. "You're in charge."

Harold was definitely the grown up. He had thinning hair and crinkles around his eyes. His chest hairs were grey. His skin reminded Ellie of the leather seats of her father's Lincoln Mark V: tan, worn out, and covered with mysterious stains.

So the Blossoms soldiered on. At least the blue path wasn't as steep as the original one. Everyone could yammer and sing. Trudy Berkowitz of the Tulips started a round of "The Ants Go Marching One by One, Hurrah" that even Ellie joined in on. It surprised Ellie that a Tulip would chose such a babyish song. But Tulips were nothing if not unpredictable.

Eventually the sounds became louder and clearer. Horns bleated. A drum thumped. An electric guitar trilled. There was no beat, but it was music. Everyone stopped singing. Like lemmings they followed Harold as he led them towards the cacophony.

Then the path ended abruptly, spilling girls onto a steep grassy hill. At the foot of the hill was a dirt road, and a big old house with a wraparound porch. Beer cans were strewn across a narrow yard in front. There was a band on the porch, hippy men like Harold, ten musicians all together, a blur of denim, ripped tee shirts, long hair, feathered hats, bandanas, and beards. Cigarettes hung from lips, hairy man-toes tapped. They all looked drowsy. Most wore dark sunglasses.

The men didn't notice the Blossoms up on the hill, girls spilled out and spread like wildflowers, shielding their eyes against the sudden blazing sun. Maybe because the girls were silent. Their jaws dropped in wonder, gangly arms at their sides. Frozen and a little scared.

Finally, a guy who looked like Dracula glanced up from his guitar and noticed them. A creepy smile spread on his face. Ellie half expected to see fangs, but all he had were yellow teeth, like Harold's. Dracula stopped strumming and made a peace sign at them. His guitar swung off his narrow shoulder from a macramé strap.

"Oh my God," gasped Debby, her hand to her mouth as if she'd seen something sudden and obscene. "It's, like, a real band."

"Duh," Beth Edelson rolled her eyes, "What a retard."

By now, other musicians had noticed the girls and stopped playing. A few waved half-heartedly. But for the most part it seemed they couldn't care less about this sudden audience. The men moved around the porch as if walking through mud, slow and deliberate, a little wobbly. They muttered to each other in low voices, laughed and shrugged, then started playing their weird music again.

"Let's give a listen." Harold made hand gestures to indicate the girls should sit down. The Tulips were thrilled. The Daisies not so. The Roses wanted to impress the Tulips, so they pretended to be cool with it. When everyone was settled, Harold sat Indian-style himself and swayed back and forth as if he were in a trance.

[119]

The music was a big snooze. Terrible, as far as Ellie was concerned. She couldn't find a beat there at all. Dracula went on string picking tangents, the drums suddenly rat-a-tat-tated. The song went on and on. And on. Time slogged on in slow motion. Ellie was bored stiff. She was starving. She was broiling hot, roasting like a chicken there in the sun. The dry grass poked her bare skin. She had to sit with her knees hunched to her chest and her arms wrapped around her shins, which was really uncomfortable and hard to do, especially on a hill angled like a ski slope.

Ellie looked around at the other Blossoms. Some were already eating their sandwiches. That seemed like a good idea, so Ellie pulled out her own soggy PB and J and started munching. A bunch of other girls lied down to sunbathe, or maybe to sleep. A few played hand games: "The Spades Go Two Lips," or "Patty Cake." Crafty types made dandelion chains and draped them on their foreheads, or long ones to hang around their necks. Whenever Ellie tried to make a dandelion-chain necklace, hers always broke, because she went overboard, got carried away with too many weeds.

But really, most of the girls looked as bored as Ellie. The only ones who seemed happy to be there were the Tulips. Joy in particular. She'd made her way down the hill and was dancing all by herself. Joy lifted her arms over her head and waved her arms all airy-fairy. She swayed her body like she was doing the hula. Ellie could see Joy's pale stomach and a bit of white underpants sticking out above her dungaree shorts.

Ellie wasn't the only one watching Joy. Dracula seemed interested also. He smiled his creepy yellow-toothed smile at Joy, and Joy wiggled her hips a little more. Gross me out, thought Ellie. She tried focusing elsewhere, but she couldn't. She polished off her sandwich and studied them; her eyes glued to the man watching the girl and the girl watching the man.

The result was a queasy tummy. Ellie looked around the hill for Lois, who usually carried Tums, along with Band Aids and Bactine. Ellie couldn't find her counselor anywhere. All she could do was hug her knees even tighter against her stomach in the hopes that would somehow soothe her nausea.

Meanwhile, Harold had joined Joy down by the side of the road. He danced like the Scarecrow from The Wizard of Oz, all discombobulated and dopey. At one point Harold crossed the road and took a super long puff of the saxophonist's cigarette. A marijuana joint, thought Ellie. She'd seen one before. Arlo and Hannah had been smoking a joint one night when Ellie's parents were out and Hannah was babysitting her. Ellie was supposed to be asleep, but she'd heard them laughing in the backyard so she went outside to see what was so funny. She'd hid behind the garage and watched the teenagers puff and puff, and get stupider and stupider. When they started

French kissing she went back to bed and tried to forget the whole scene.

Finally the music stopped. Hallelujah, thought Ellie. The Blossoms could go back to the woods now, where it was cool and hushed, where there wasn't a hippy band, and Tulips weren't trying to act older than they really were. Ellie stood up, sweaty and sunburned, her joints stiff. Other Blossoms stood as well, stretching creaky arms upwards, brushing dirt and grass from their rompers and shorts.

But Harold was still busy, taking tokes and chugging beer, all buddy-buddy with the band.

"Let's get truckin', Harold," screamed Debby.

All the Blossoms mumbled in agreement, but no one gave Debby credit for speaking up.

Harold looked up at the girls as if he'd just remembered they were there. As he tried to focus on them with bloodshot, droopy eyes, Dracula started playing the guitar.

"If I fell in love with you, would you promise to be true..." Dracula's voice was beastly, not anything like Paul McCartney's.

"...and help me understand..."

More like he'd stuffed his mouth with Red Hots and was trying to spit them out.

"...cause I've been in love before and I found that love was more..."

"...than just holding hands." This came from Joy, sung in her deep molasses voice as she crossed the road and climbed onto the porch. She picked up a tambourine and slapped at it as if she'd been born with it in her hand.

Together Joy and Dracula sang "If I trust in you..." The girl's voice sweetened the man's, like syrup over spiced sausage.

The men on the porch looked as if something had smacked them out of their stupors. Their eyes widened, their spines straightened. The Blossoms were speechless and still. Everyone saw what Ellie had already seen: Joy and Dracula together were perfect and creepy at the same time.

Finally, the love song ended. Girls shifted on the hill uncomfortably, and men shuffled in place and looked at their feet. It was time for Joy to cross back over and join her campmates, but she stayed put. She giggled as Dracula leaned towards her, put his hand to her cheek.

Ellie looked over at Debby, hoping she'd say or do something. Something Debby-dopey, something loud. But Debby just stood there like everyone else, mouth opened like a grouper fish. It was up to Ellie to break the spell that settled over everyone, men and girls alike.

"Arrrgggh," Ellie yelled, like a pirate. She noisily crumpled the tinfoil around her leftover sandwich crusts and shoved it all in her daypack.

"Anyone wanna take a swim?" A new voice pierced the thick air. "Swimming hole is around back." It

[123]

was the fattest hippy, a guy who'd been playing the trombone. Dark sweat stains spread in a blobby pattern across the tight tee shirt that girdled his belly.

Swimming had been Ellie's original mission. There was nothing more that she'd wanted to do on this dismal day. It had been her birthday quest. A swimming hole sounded much better than a shallow stream. Not quite Waterfront, but still. Without much thinking she cried out "I do!"

"Groovy," Fatso nodded. "Come and join the party." The band staggered off the porch and disappeared behind the house. Dracula took Joy's hand, and together they followed.

Harold looked up at Ellie and smiled in sloppy approval. Then he crossed the road and disappeared as well. All that remained were girls, Blossoms, huddled around Ellie like she was some kind of leader. They gaped at her in amazement. Ellie was more shocked by her outburst than any of them, but she wasn't going to let on.

"Grab your pack, Debby," said Ellie as she picked up her own.

"Huh?" said Debby.

Ellie gestured towards the woods. "We can change back in there. They won't be able to see us."

Boldly she trudged back into the woods. Debby followed. The rest stayed put, caught in the betwixt and betweenness that had defined the entire day. Losers, thought Ellie. Scaredy cats.

Ellie and Debby changed in a hurry, as if they didn't rush they might lose their nerve. They ripped off grass-stained clothes and squeezed sweaty body parts into bathing suits. Ellie's ruffled two-piece top left welts on her skinny shoulders. Debby's tank suit wedged up her butt crack.

When they emerged, the other girls watched them proceed down the hill, two barefoot emissaries from Planet Girl. Dry grass and rocks poked and pinched Ellie's feet, but she kept her stride as steady as she could. She looked both ways before crossing the dusty road, like she'd been taught to do at a very early age. Then she realized how dumb it was, as there hadn't been a car in sight all day.

"Do you think I can pee in the water without anyone knowing?" Debby asked as they walked past the porch.

"Gross, Debby," Ellie barked, though she herself had peed in just about every body of water she'd ever been in.

As they rounded the house, the setting sun hit Ellie's eyes with blinding fierceness. She heard splashing and saw the glistening surface of water. One high pitched girlish laugh punctuated a mess of manly chuckles and slurry words.

Ellie's eyes adjusted. The swimming hole was a disappointing, murky pond. Most of the band sat in shallow water, sloshing water up their arms like kids in puddles after a rainstorm. Joy and Dracula were off by themselves.

Debby gasped. "Look! Joy's wearing her bra." Debby broke into uncontrollable hiccup-y giggles, as if someone was tickling the soles of her feet.

Ellie had to squint to see it. Joy's bra was the kind with wires and hooks and all that other stuff that real bosoms required. The kind Ellie's mother wore. It was wet and see-through. Joy's big nipples visible behind decorative lace. Her panties were the same kind Ellie wore. High-waisted Carter's briefs. Wetness made them see-through. Between Joy's chubby thighs, a dark shock.

Dracula had been crouching in the water. Now he rose. Sludgy pond water dripped from his body. His naked body. His penis dangled between hairy man-legs, long, thick, and fleshy.

Ellie had never seen a grown-up penis before. This penis wasn't like the little knobs boy babies had. It had nothing in common with the smooth pencil-thin penises that poked out of boys' bathing suits at Waterfront every now and then. This penis was ugly. Stupid looking. Pink, but not nice pink. Dusty, chewed up bubble gum pink. Undercooked pork pink.

This was a mess of strangeness. Ellie's queasy stomach returned. Seeing a grown man's penis wasn't on her birthday wish list. She hadn't ever really wondered about grown men's penises, but now one had been forced upon her psyche. 'This is what I have to look forward to,' she thought.

"Ew, yuck." Debby said, as if reading Ellie's mind. But Debby wasn't looking at Dracula. She was gaping at a trio of band members who had also risen from the depths. The men were in their own world, staggering in the water, bumbling and unstable. Naked. Each one had his own hairy penis. One hung lopsidedly. Another was short and thick like a bottle stopper. The third was even longer than Dracula's. They were all pretty gross. Dangly, wobbly, wrinkled, snaky things. Alien creatures glommed on to the men's bodies, swingy happily between their host's hips.

The men barely noticed the emissaries from Planet Girl, which was a good thing. Still, all this nakedness made Ellie sick to her stomach. PB and J, and Hi-C churned in her guts. Her mouth filled with saliva. Ellie willed herself to look down at the grass beneath her feet. A tiny frog stood by her right big toe. The sides of its torso pulsed, as if it were trying desperately to hold itself together, hoping this gigantic creature hovering above would leave it alone, that soon it would be free to hop away and resume life as it was.

Ellie stared at the frog as Joy and Dracula splashed out of the pond and walked past her towards the big house. It wasn't until a creaky door open and shut with a loud crack that the frog hopped away, making a frenzied, zig-zaggy mad dash. But Ellie remained still. Head down. Her own sides heaving. Pulsing.

"Dan-ger Will Ro-bin-son," Debby said robotically. "Joy Kra-mer in big tro-uble, affirmative?"

Ellie didn't move.

Debby poked Ellie's arm. "Earth to Ellie, you still wanna go swimming?"

"What? Are you retarded?" Ellie snapped. "You're such a moron." Ellie ran away from the stupid pond. All these ugly, hairy penises thrust upon her on her birthday. Joy and Dracula. Everything was unfair.

Ellie rounded the house and trudged up the hill through the tall scratchy grass. Daisies, Roses, and Tulips huddled together shivering and rubbing their legs to stay warm in the dying daylight. As Ellie approached, they yelled out questions, pleaded for juicy tidbits, but Ellie ignored them. She sat off by herself in her dry bathing suit, stunned and unable to touch her own skin. Let Debby tell them if she wants, she thought. Who cares anyway?

The sun was setting behind the hill. Blossoms hunkered low, cloaked in darkness. No one knew what to do. They sat like miserable stones, an ancient ruin in the mysterious dusk.

Just as a bunch of Blossoms broke into sobs, the camp bus came careening down the dirt road, screeching to a halt in front of the house. As dust swirled behind it in a dismal haze, the door flapped open, and out came Camp

Director Myrna, followed by sturdier counselor Lois. Ellie would eventually learn that her ever-responsible counselor had hitchhiked back to camp and told Myrna about Harold's "inappropriate detour." But that would be the next day. Right then all Ellie knew was that this had been the lamest, weirdest, grossest, stupidest, most important birthday she'd ever had.

Myrna looked up at her campers and sheepishly called "Who Ha Ha...Who Ha Ha..."

No one returned the Camp Lakawalla call. Myrna looked like she expected and deserved a million pies to be thrown at her frowny face.

Then the front door of the house opened. The remaining sunlight shone down on the porch like a spotlight. As if on cue, out walked Joy, fully clothed but markedly changed. Something askew. Her face looked like the porcelain harlequin mask Ellie's grandmother had hanging in her guest powder room. Same rigid grimace, ghostly but glistening pallor, explicitly rosy cheeks.

The next morning, Joy's parents would arrive at Camp Lakawalla and quietly, without a fuss, take their daughter home. Harold would already be gone, gone, gone. It drove Ellie bananas that everyone talked at breakfast about the Nature Hike in hushed, excited tones, as if it had been a racy hot-headed adventure for everyone. Ellie knew for a fact most of the girls had been bored to tears, sunburned, and starved. None of them had even gotten off their butts to wander behind the house for a swim. None of them had seen what Ellie had seen. Penises that would mark the day. Penises and Joy, with her teenage bosom and wild side. None of them.

Stranger in Paradise

The beach is empty at dawn. The angle of the coarse, crumbling sand undoes Helen's gait. She's not used to walking barefoot. She's jet-lagged and wilted due to the humidity and heat. Her flight from O'Hare had been delayed two hours, which meant two hours of uncomfortable wakefulness on a hard bench by the gate before she'd even boarded the plane. The only remedy had been to pop a Valium once airborne, and chase it down with a G and T from the flight attendant's rolling cart of liquid goodies.

6 a.m., and Helen is still woozy. She's wearing a gauzy caftan over her sporty tankini, but she feels naked, exposed. The rising tropical sun already blazes with an intensity that shocks, feels dangerous. Helen has sunscreen in her canvas tote, along with a paperback novel and a towel. She'll put some on once she's found a place to settle.

She also has her baggie of ashes. The smidgen of John she carries everywhere, still, even after a year of widowhood. She keeps the baggie in a smooth silk pouch when she's out and about. But sometimes in private she takes John out and looks through the plastic at his flecks of bone, his grey dust, his odd leftover clumps. Sometimes she combs through him with her fingers.

Helen slips and slides her way along the lopsided beach, when she sees a surfer at the water's edge. Helen's never seen a real surfer before. She and John never took beach vacations, preferring cultural European or Asian excursions when time and money allowed. This surfer spotting is exciting, yet Helen hesitates. They are the only two people on the beach, and this loads the moment even more. She shivers in spite of the swampy air.

The surfer turns in her direction just as Helen hugs herself in an attempt to quell the shakes. He's an assault of color: blond and ridiculously tan; the surfboard, fire engine red; his bathing shorts, neon blue.

"Hey there," he calls, waving. His arm's ropy and rippled; his torso, muscled and bulky.

Helen gives a little finger wiggle in return.

He beckons her. "Don't worry. I don't bite." He's got a broad American-but-unplaceable accent that Helen finds both inviting and assaultive.

Don't be such a timid fool, Helen tells herself. Go on. She approaches, trying to look dignified as she trudges through the sand.

"Welcome to Paradise," he reaches his hand towards her when she's near enough. "I'm Jules."

He's a tropical Jack LaLanne, with grey-blond dreads, darkened leathery skin, defined sinews, and gleaming white teeth. He's as old as I am, Helen thinks. Maybe even older.

"I'm Helen." She takes his hand, which is dry, calloused and warm as summer pavement.

"You must've come in on the red-eye," Jules nods sagely. His eyes are blue, almost as neon as his shorts. The whites are not quite white, though. There's an unhealthy yellowish tinge. "Bet you feel like shit."

"Well, not my finest hour," Helen shrugs, suddenly aware of how on the edge she is. She could collapse on the beach right now and sleep for days.

Jules drops his board and crouches next to it, pats it like a pet. "Best cure for jet lag, hangovers, insomnia, you name it, right here." He begins rubbing the surfboard with a palm-sized bar of wax.

"I could never surf," Helen sighs. "I can barely swim."

Jules shoves the wax in a Velcro pocket by his toned butt cheek. "Never say never, Helen of Troy." Jules stands and hoists the board under his arm. He's nearly naked, and so close to her she could lick his belly button. "The world is your oyster." Jules winks, then dashes to the ocean. He catapults onto his surfboard like a flying angel, his wild-haired head high, his arms paddling furiously through the water, the muscles in his back tensing and pulsing like a claymation puppet.

Helen is alone again. She could keep walking and see what else lies ahead. She could return to her lovely hotel room with its broad, comfortable bed, crisp 400 thread count sheets, silent air conditioning, and balcony with sweeping views. Or she could stay and watch Jules surf.

That wink, she wonders. Was it flirtatious or merely friendly?

What else is there to do, really? She lays her towel down, fidgeting to find a comfortable position that doesn't hurt her back, or expose her varicose veins. She takes out her sunscreen and dabs it on all exposed body parts. Eventually she leans back on her elbows with her legs straight out, ankles crossed demurely, the gauzy caftan draped over the worst of the spidery blue lines on her thighs.

Watching Jules surf is not as exciting as she'd hoped it would be. In fact, it is deadly dull. Mostly he sits out there, bobbing up and down like a human cork. But every now and then a wave rolls in from the horizon in a swelling onslaught. Jules paddles towards it and suddenly he's standing, careening across the wave, his surfboard like a needle piercing and embellishing the wave until it turns to white foam and disappears as if it never existed in the first place.

Eventually other surfers arrive: young men, who strut past Helen like peacocks. They stretch and yell and curse for each other, and for a gaggle of half-dressed girls who also stumble to the beach, collapsing in a giggling, hungover pile. Some hold lidded coffees, others clutch beers.

This whole mess of twentysomething display is only a few yards to Helen's left, but no one notices Helen, which suits her fine. She's used to the slow seepage of middle-aged inconsequence. Mostly her invisibility is a joyful relief. She can wander everywhere, like a ghost.

But Jules noticed her. Granted, they had been the only ones on the beach, and it would've been extremely weird for them not to have acknowledged each other. Still, most men his age only had eyes for women young enough to be their daughters.

Helen feels a clutching in her chest as she thinks about Jules' handshake, his gleaming white smile, his parting wink. She watches as he catches another wave, a giant blue monster that seems to toy with him as he twists and turns and thrusts his hips to stay upright. Helen's heart palpitations get worse. She reaches inside her tote to caress John's baggie. She fingers the silk pouch, prodding the fabric, making sure John is safe and snug inside.

Meanwhile, the younger surfers go through variations of the same pre-surf ritual; the rubbing of the boards, the thrusty, callisthenic stretches. Then they career like a flock of seagulls into the ocean. These youngsters are swift. They jockey for position, cutting Jules off, stealing waves from him. He's invisible out there, obsolete, like Helen is here on land.

[135]

Soon after he's been crowded out, Jules paddles back towards the shore and ambles up the sand. Helen sits upright, recrosses her legs, and spreads her caftan over her pasty flesh.

"Helen of Troy! You're still here." Jules gasps. He's short of breath.

We're neither of us, spring chickens, thinks Helen.

"I thought I'd stay and watch," she says. She averts her eyes as he hovers over her, seawater dripping off his body, his bathing trunks, his snaky hair. "I hope that's okay."

Jules grins like the Cheshire Cat. "More than okay."

"You did great out there," Helen warbles. She sounds like a rain-drenched pigeon. She hasn't been this physically close to a man since she sat by John's bed watching him die, holding his chilly hand, which in the end was more like a bony claw. "I've never seen real surfing before. It's all so, so...dramatic."

"Ha! Dramatic. Now ain't that the truth." Jules laughs and plops down on the sand next to her. He smells like a fetid swamp creature. Helen assumes this is the way all surfers smell after surfing. Sweaty. Slightly sour.

Helen can feel her cheeks aflame. The clutching in her chest is now a rapid pulse. She stands and gathers her belongings. "I really have to get back to the hotel and go to sleep. It was really nice meeting you, Jules."

"Come back at sunset, Queen Helen. I'll be surfing the evening glass off. We have a little party at the end of each day."

Who are 'we'? Helen wonders. Is Jules married? Is this not really flirting after all?

"I don't know," she hesitates.

"There'll be booze and some food. You'll meet great people."

Helen hoists her tote onto her shoulder. She reaches in with her free hand to make sure John is safe in his pouch. "Maybe. Probably. We'll see."

"See you later, Helen of Troy." Jules lifts his hand towards her, and she reaches hers to meet it. He kisses her knuckles with wet, plump lips.

Helen feels like an infidel, the same hand having just been with her husband. A sudden chill spider-walks up her spine.

+++++++

Images of Jules and his dripping dreads, his smarmy yet seductive smile, his athleticism, kept coming back to Helen all afternoon like a nagging headache, which was why she chose not to join him and his compadres for their sunset hullabaloo. Instead she watches this miracle of nature alone on her deck with an overpriced minibar bourbon on the rocks watering down on the rattan ottoman by her side. The sunset is astonishing. A ball of fire descending through godlike clouds before fizzling to a pulse behind the cobalt sea.

Later, Helen feels a tinge of regret. She's restless in bed, can't sleep. Thoughts collect like a pile of damp laundry in need of another hot tumble. Am I a killjoy? What am I so scared of? Jules was just being friendly. This is a missed opportunity. Maybe it's time, as the saying goes, to step out of my comfort zone.

And so the next evening, while there's still a dusting of light in the sky, after a full resort-centric day including restorative yoga class on the hotel's private beach, a brief spritz in the Jacuzzi, a nap, and a shower, Helen decides she'll go back to the beach and see what's going on.

Helen arranges her thick, naturally chestnut hair, still a source of middle-aged pride, in a loose ponytail. She coats her lips in 'Calypso Coral.' Not her usual shade, but the pinkish-orange hue seems appropriate to the occasion and location. She looks past the crêpey folds of her neck and the furrows lining her forehead. She's still relatively attractive. And everything after a certain age is relative.

"Off we go," she says to her reflection. Helen places John's silk pouch in her zippered windbreaker pocket and leaves her room in search of...what?

+++++++

There's a bonfire, bongos, a ukulele, bottles of rum, the stink of meat roasting on a spit. A riotous mob dances, mostly young women in sarongs and bare-chested young men. They gyrate and writhe. Hips rotate and shake. Necks stretch and wobble. Arms sway and fists pump. There are older people also dancing, but they look idiotic. Helen feels embarrassed watching her peers, thin-haired, saggy-skinned and stiff, attempt to join the ritualistic chaos. They look like clumsy marionettes. On the perimeter of this madness Helen notices a wrinkled bald man with a machete cracking open coconuts and handing them to anyone who walks past. If not for his white beard and tattooed forearms, he's a dead ringer for Ira Kapolwitz, Helen's dentist back home.

Over by a spiky bush, Jules plays the bongos with his eyes shut as if he's praying, rocking forward and back, side to side. Next to Jules is a ukulele player, a striking giant with broad, gnarled features that harken back to indigenous roots. He's quite good, plucking and strumming sweet tinny notes with marvelous ease. Jules, however, is only so-so. He keeps the beat, but barely. The ukulele player seems oblivious to Jules' clunky pounding. It's possible he's too plastered to notice.

Helen finds a tree stump to sit on and tries to blend in. She sways as best she can to the almost beat of Jules bongo. This is fun, she tells herself. This is authentic. This is exotic. It helps that John's there inside the silk pouch, deep in the zipped pocket of her windbreaker.

When something furry rubs up against Helen's bare calf, she shrieks and stands abruptly. A ratty mutt with red-rimmed eyes and brown, bottle-bristled fur stares up at her wagging a stumpy tail. One ear is flopped over, scarred and torn, the other upright and intact.

It is only when Jules calls out, "Ah, Helen of Troy! You made it!" that Helen realizes the music has stopped and all eyes, bleary and unfocused as they may be, are on her. She shrugs, which causes the dog to bark, which in turn causes Helen to startle again and totter backwards. She almost falls, but only almost. She rights herself in time to save her dignity.

Jules rises from his bongos and makes his way over to her. She's relieved to see that nobody else is paying attention to her anymore. The ukulele player has wandered off to talk to the Ira look-a-like. Others— young, old, black, brown, pasty, sunburned—sip out of red Solo cups and engage in slurred conversations.

"I see you've met Champo," Jules says as he crouches by Helen's thigh. His large fingers dig in behind the mutt's ears. The dog's tongue dangles off to the side of its mouth while its little tail wags in obscene canine bliss.

"Is he yours?" Helen asks.

"Champo belongs to everyone..." Jules pauses and smiles up at Helen, his perfect piano key teeth a-dazzle in the bonfire glow. "...and no one."

Jules releases his grip from Champo's skull, and the dog runs off in search of someone or something else to satisfy his urges. Jules stands, and Helen gets a whiff of pungent body odor, which tonight is layered with a strong slam of Old Spice.

"Come on," Jules wraps an arm around Helen's shoulder. Very buddy-buddy. "I'm wicked thirsty."

And so they drink. Jules fills Helen's Solo cup with a rum concoction. It's a syrupy, sweet brew, not Helen's kind of cocktail, but she downs it gamely. They wander among the other partiers, and Jules introduces her as "Helen of Troy." Everyone else has a nickname too: Tazer Man, Butchy Boy, Morning Star, El Jefe, Sarge, Hail Britannia, Ellie Bellie. The Ira-look alike goes by the moniker of Blaze.

The night slides along, and Helen slides with it. She laughs at crass jokes. She compliments tacky jewelry. She sings along to '70s hits she didn't like in the '70s. She drinks some more. She's been drunker in this past year of mourning. She's drowned her sorrow, collapsed on her empty bed on multiple occasions in a whirl of nausea and numbness. This feels different, though, an intoxicating blend of desperation and freedom. Look at me, she thinks, I'm on a beach surrounded by towering palm trees and gargantuan plants that look like mutations. I'm partying with the party people. She watches a pesky monkey snatch a hat off Hail Britannia's head. It might just be the rum that makes her feel this is all a hoot. But Helen doesn't care. It's about time she had a little fun.

+++++++

Hours into the night, Helen finds herself sitting on a scratchy blanket with Jules. She's only a few yards from the frenzied, boisterous fun, but it feels like she's miles away. She's been revealing her personal history in dribs and drabs. She's given away the basics: Midwesterner, former schoolteacher, then a wife and mother, now a widow and long-distance parent. Jules is vague about his personal details, and quickly returns the focus to Helen.

"You're good people, Helen of Troy." He takes her hand. His is sweaty. "An upright citizen. I could tell the moment I met you."

She glides her hand away to sip her third—or is it fourth?—rum punch. Helen laughs. "Good people...well maybe. But right now I'm not feeling all that upright."

"Cheers." Jules raises his cup. "Here's to the lopsided among us!"

They press their plastic tumblers together in a dull clack. Jules glugs his as if it were a breakfast smoothie. Helen knows better, but still, she takes a few hearty swigs of her own.

They talk some more, or rather Jules does. Helen is quite tipsy; the best she can do is nod and attempt to follow his monologue. Jules shares local lore: surf culture, colonial history, agriculture, expat goldmines in real estate and coffee.

A bit later, they are lying on their backs pointing out constellations to each other. Helen spots Orion's Belt. Jules finds the easy-to-locate Little Dipper. It seems friendly and chaste. But if it were to turn in to something more? Well maybe that wouldn't be so terrible, Helen decides. Maybe it's about time.

"Tell me a secret," Jules says, turning on his side and grinning down at her with his feline grin. "Something no one else knows. And I'll tell you mine."

"I don't have any secrets," Helen says, which is something she honestly believes.

"Everyone has secrets. I'll go first. Mine's a show and tell." He turns away from her and fiddles around with something close to his face. He turns back and smiles again, only this time his mouth is a gaping, toothless maw.

Helen gasps. She's horrified.

Jules holds his dentures up in his palm proudly. Then he snaps them back in his mouth and laughs. "Bad genes and too much candy as a kid. There's not a person in my family over fifty with a full set of chompers."

Helen regains her composure enough to say, "I'm sorry."

"No need to be," Jules shrugs. "I look better with my movie star teeth. The originals were as crooked as a posse of Wall Street lawyers. Okay, now it's your turn. Time to spill the beans."

+++++++

Helen lifts her head, and grains of sand tumble down the side of her face. Her tongue is a salted slab, her temples pound as if an angry gnome wants out of her head. As her eyes adjust to the foggy dimness, Helen realizes it is dawn, that she's fallen asleep on the beach.

She's not alone. There are bodies everywhere, fetally curled or with arms and legs akimbo. Stray dogs—Champo among them—sniff crotches and paw through food scraps. Jules lies next to Helen, snoring in disjointed spurts, his mouth agape, his fake teeth gleaming like a ring of pearls.

Helen has a hazy memory of divulged secrets, vulnerabilities, regrets. Nothing sexual occurred. That, at least, she's sure of. She stands up, careful not to wake Jules, and slips away.

Back at the hotel, she places John's ashes, snug still in the silk pouch, atop the mini-fridge and manages to strip out of her sandy, booze-infused clothing. After showering off the residue of her crazy night, Helen rubs her wet hair briskly with the plush hotel towel. Grains of sand remain embedded near her scalp. Two shampoo rinses, and still they're as stubborn as head lice.

Helen examines her reflection in the steamy bathroom mirror. Her skin is shockingly sallow and her eyes are bloodshot. After so much picking and rubbing, her hair shoots out in a wild circus of unattractive tangles.

"The party is over," Helen says definitively as she turns away from herself and tries to imagine how she'll manage for the rest of the day.

+++++++

[144]

Just as Helen considers leaving for a hair-of-the-dog in the hotel bar, her room phone rings assaultively at 5 p.m. A surge of stomach acid worms its way towards her throat. "What is it? What's wrong?" She gasps. She's been conditioned to expect bad news from unexpected phone calls.

"Nada, Helen of Troy," Jules' voice is a chipper assault. "No problemos. Sarge is taking us out on his schooner. We're going on a sunset cruise."

She's told herself she's had enough. What she really needs is a bromide and a bland meal. But she's heading back home the next afternoon, and a sunset cruise sounds so benign and such a lovely way to end her vacation.

"Come on. It's gonna be a killer sunset," Jules says with the ease of a radio announcer.

He's drawn her in. "Well, if you insist."

"I do insist! Indeed I do," Jules says and then adds, "Hey, we may get a little wet. It might be best to leave John behind."

And then it comes back to her, the thing she revealed, her secret. She'd shown Jules her baggie full of ashes in the wee dark hours of the morning. He'd asked to hold them. Jules studied John solemnly, reverently. He nodded and said, "Thank you, so, so much," before handing him back.

Helen puts the receiver down. She walks over to the silk pouch and fondles it for a moment. The ashes

[145]

within clump and give, clump and give. She takes the baggie out. A tiny bit of bone pokes her thumb. She knows better than to prod too forcefully, lest the shard rip the baggie and cause catastrophic spillage.

Leave John behind, she thinks. I can do this.

Helen puts the baggie back in the pouch atop the mini-fridge and gathers her things. Waiting for the elevator she has a moment of regret about leaving John behind. Like a child she thinks, Jules isn't the boss of me. She's about to turn back to get the pouch when the elevator door slides open. A pool-bound family of four stare at Helen impatiently while she hesitates. As the doors begin to close, Helen thrusts herself inside. She's acutely aware of her empty pocket, the lack of subtle pressure against her thigh, of ashes to flesh.

Jules is leaning against the check-in counter, deep in conversation with Cesar, the head concierge. His dreads are tied up in a man-bun, and he's wearing a pectoral-hugging black spandex tee shirt. Both men smile broadly as Helen approaches.

"Bonita, bonita," Jules nods, eying her from top to bottom.

"Si, si," Cesar agrees.

"Come on Helen of Troy," Jules grabs her elbow and rushes her along the slick tile floor towards the exit. "The gang awaits."

+++++++

Butchy Boy, Morning Star, and El Jefe are also along for the trip. Turquoise water slaps against the sides of the boat, which is small but comfortable, like a floating living room. Helen's a bit tipsy and the boat is the same. She's mesmerized by another tropical sunset, a spectacular shift of pinks and oranges and fire. She sips her rum and eats ceviche so tart with lime her mouth smolders. She watches Morning Star dance, nymph-like, while El Jefe sings a song. Helen understands a few words—corazon, mi amor, muerte—and feels appropriately forlorn.

They bob out there for hours. Helen nods off at some point, but wakes as the boat docks shortly before midnight. Jules walks her back to the hotel. Along the way he tells her local gossip. Divorces. Affairs. Out of wedlock half-native children. But no personal details. Jules is Teflon.

In the lobby, Helen wonders if she should invite Jules up to her room, go the whole nine yards, throw even more caution to the wind. If he stayed the night, would he take out his teeth and soak them in a glass of water? What would their bodies even be capable of at this age, after this much booze? But before Helen even has the chance to say something, if indeed she were to say something, Jules beats her to the chase.

"Well Helen of Troy, it's been great hanging with you," He grabs both her shoulders firmly with his arms extended, like a dad taking stock of a child who's about to go off to college. "I hope you have a great life."

So that's it, she thinks, realizing it is for the best. To go any further with this odd, evasive man, a man with false teeth who wears spandex, a man who ties his hair up in a bun and plays the bongos; this could spell disaster. She finds her voice. "You too, Jules. I hope your life is spectacular."

Back in her room, Helen changes out of soggy clothes. Too tired to shower, she puts on pajamas, quickly douses her face with warm water from the bathroom tap and brushes the residue of booze and fish from her mouth. Finally Helen nestles deep in the center of the enormous bed, overwhelmed by the pitch and wooze of her night. She tosses and turns, tries to settle, but can't.

Helen gets out of bed and grabs John's ashes, which are still atop the mini-fridge. She carries the pouch back to bed and places it under her pillow. Penance. A lumpy reminder. Eventually she drifts off to sleep.

+++++++

In spite of a massive headache and a sour stomach on the verge of exploding, Helen gets to the airport early. She'd heard that getting through customs can be a slog. She's barely walked through the screening device when a security guard comes up to her and asks in clipped English, "Did any persons approach you to take a package for them?"

"Of course not," Helen huffs. "I would never." Then she sees her belongings at the end of the conveyor belt being pawed through by TSA personnel. She stands there in her socks, awash with sudden dread. Before she knows it, two guards whisk Helen away, grabbing her roughly by the elbows while two others collect her carry-on bag, her shoes, and her coat.

"Where are you taking me?" she asks, her voice meek, like a shoeless child being led to a time out.

The guards ignore her. They won't look her in the eye. They talk to each other across her, uttering clipped words: mule, vieja, estupido. The last one she understands.

"I am not stupid!" she cries.

They push through a door that says NO ENTRADA and pull her down a grimy hallway lit by faulty fluorescents that flicker and threaten to die. There are multiple doors along the hallway, each one painted a glaring orange, each with a window placed too high for Helen to look through.

"Aqui," the guard holding her coat says, indicating a specific room with a thrust of his grizzled chin. Inside there's a long table, some folding chairs. The guard pulls out a chair and says to Helen, "You sit here."

Helen does as told. She's trembling. The room is overly air-conditioned, and it makes her quaking all the worse. Combined with her hangover it feels like she has a terrible flu, like she might vomit all over the cracked and filthy linoleum tabletop.

The grizzly guard looks at her with dead eyes. Then he turns to the other guards and speaks rapidly in Spanish, and there's not a word Helen can make out. He and two others exit, leaving one behind, the only woman of the bunch, the one who had squeezed Helen's left elbow so tightly Helen is sure there will be a bruise. The guard looks barely out of her teens. She's short and built like a bulldog, with ebony hair slicked back in a temple-tugging bun. She stands in the corner of the room with her arms crossed under large breasts. A heavy belt, with gun, handcuffs, and other tortuous-looking devices hangs around her non-existent waist.

If this mess isn't cleared up soon Helen will miss her plane, but there's nothing for her to do but shiver and fret. She gazes at posters lining one wall of the room. Mug shots of scary looking thieves, fruits and vegetables with large red Xs across them. At the end of the wall is a poster of powders. Grayish piles, brownish piles, whitish piles. Under these photos is the word HEROINA.

Beneath the grayish pile it could just as easily say JOHN.

Helen understands. There's been a terrible mistake.

"They're not drugs!" She yells at the guard. "They're my husband's ashes. I'm allowed to carry them.

It's perfectly legal. I have my cremation certificate. It's in my bag. I can show it to you."

But the young guard won't look at her.

"Por favor," Helen pounds the table. "Please, listen!"

The stubborn girl widens her stance and stares off at a spot a few inches past Helen's right shoulder.

Helen sighs. When the head guard comes back she'll explain. She looks at the photo of the uncut drugs, that grayish powder which eerily resemble her husband's remains. And then it comes to her, washes over her like a sudden fever. Jules, she thinks. His fascination with John's ashes. How he said, "Thank you" before handing them back to her at the beach party, like she'd given him a gift. Jules switched John's ashes with drugs, heroina right there in her Le Sportsac carry-on tote.

She remembers Jules' easy way with Cesar. How Jules had said "It might be best to leave John behind." She's sure Cesar went up to her room while Jules had her out on the boat. Cesar switched John for heroin. And the rest of them. They were all in on it. The whole lot, with their idiotic nicknames and boozy ways. She imagines there's yet another accomplice somewhere along the way, maybe even in this airport. Someone lying in wait to pounce and then sweet talk Helen into more reckless behavior, to con her, and swipe the drugs while she was in oblivious submission.

Helen's been duped. She's a patsy. And now she's being watched like a hawk by a teenage girl with a gun. She collapses forward, her forehead on the sticky table top. She starts to sob, wailing like she hasn't in months. Minutes pass. Many minutes, and then the door opens and the bearded guard with the blank eyes enters. Helen pops out of her seat.

"I've had nothing to do with this," she yells, "I was set up, believe me. It was all Jules. Jules and his gang of fools!"

"Please, sit," he says. The please is extraneous. The sit is a command, so Helen does as told. The guard sits across from her and takes out a notebook and a pencil that has been chewed on and is missing the eraser.

"Who is Jules?" he asks.

"Jules, the surfer. From the beach."

"This is a true name?"

"How the hell would I know?" Helen resists the urge to grab him by the shoulders and shake some sense in to him. "Jules is the one who fooled me. He seduced me. He switched my husband's ashes for heroin."

The guard looks at her, and finally his face has expression. He looks confused. "Ashes for heroin?"

"Yes. In the baggie. In the silk pouch. He took them. He stole my John. God knows what toilet he's been flushed down."

The guard rubs his chin. Helen can almost hear his stubble swish like brush bristles.

[152]

"He's gone. John is gone," Helen moans and begins to sob again. She puts her head back down and thinks: Take me to prison. What's left for me anyway? I'm a pathetic naive idiot who can't survive on her own.

She hears the shuffle of a chair, a brief nonsensical exchange, the door open and shut. Helen raises her head and sees she's been left with the fat and unfriendly girl guard who now, at least, returns Helen's gaze. Though she's doing so while fondling the handcuffs hanging by her right hip.

More minutes pass. Helen is in a state of intense distress, her heart palpitating, her palms sweating, her breath shallow. Her world is a topsy-turvy place filled with funhouse mirrors and hidden landmines. It has been at least an hour when a new guard comes in with a tray of food for Helen. A meager serving of rice and beans, a pathetic looking chicken breast with puckered skin, a Coke, and some withered grapes. Helen picks at her meal, finds it hard to swallow. She's desperate for a drink, a real drink, but assumes asking for one would be bad form.

A phone call, she thinks. My legal right. I can ask for that, at least.

"I want to make a call," she says to the guard.

The guard shrugs in an I-don't-understand sort of way.

Helen makes the universal gesture of thumb-to-ear and pinky-to-mouth. "Telefono?"

[153]

The guard shakes her head. "No. No es posible." She shifts her stance yet again, and stares off into space.

+++++++

Someone shakes Helen's shoulder. In spite of, or because of her dire circumstances, she's managed to drift off to sleep.

"Pardon, Missus?"

She looks up at a man wearing a crisp white shirt with a large TSA badge on his chest and official TSA epaulets.

"Yes?" Helen manages, disoriented, out of sorts. She's drooled on the table and there's spittle coating her lower lip.

"There's been a terrible mistake." The man sits down across from her and holds the silk pouch aloft, like Jules held his dentures that first night, like an offering, a gift. "We've never had this kind of situation before. Here are your dear husband's ashes back. Please accept our apology. The drug trade has ruined many lives down here. We can't take chances."

Helen grabs John and holds him to her chest. The silk is sticky against her clammy skin. She's tempted to peek inside, make sure every last bone and charred bit of him is there, but it's too intimate a gesture to perform in front of this contrite stranger.

"The next flight isn't until morning, but if you'd like, we will put you up overnight at an airport hotel, courtesy of the airline," the man says. And then, as if to sweeten the deal he adds, "Dinner and drink vouchers at the hotel will be provided." As if that makes it any better.

Her belongings are by the door. She's free to go. The mini-van to the airport hotel is waiting curbside.

"Unless you have another choice of where to spend the night," says the man.

"Ha!" Helen barks. "I've got choices galore." She rises swiftly, her legs like wobbly pins, grabs her belongings and runs from the room.

+++++++

Before she leaves the airport Helen dumps a small pinch of John in the airport toilet and watches the clump dissolve. A tiny bone shard floats in the grayish pool before sinking. Her heart stops— literally stops, she's sure—when she pushes the lever and watches it swirl down the drain. At least now I know which toilet he's been flushed down, she thinks. Her heart starts again and pulses to a different beat. Maybe a better beat, maybe crazier, maybe calmer. Helen doesn't know yet.

+++++++

Helen strides down the beach at dusk. It may be her last night in paradise, or the first of many to come. She's allowed to not know. She's allowed to decide everything on a whim. Helen sees the bonfire flames in the distance, hears the uneven fwump fwump of Jules' bad bongos. She walks in the other direction.

"I've got choices galore," she says aloud for a second time that day, this time to herself. The horizon is a tangerine sizzle. Above it, darkness threatens. Soon it will be difficult to see anything but shadows.

Helen finds a place at the shoreline where her feet can sink in the sand and feel anchored when the water rolls in and churns around her ankles before sucking back out to sea. She needs to be sturdy for what's ahead.

Helen reaches in to her pocket for the baggie. She scoops out a handful of John and is about to toss him into the sea, but stops. This is not what she's compelled to do. She's Helen of Troy, Warrior Queen. Hers should be a mightier ritual.

And so Helen spreads John's ashes all over her skin, rubs clumps in her hair, daps bits in between her breasts, and behind her ears like perfume. She crunches on bits of bone as if they are stale candies. Smudges of ash decorate her face like war paint. Eventually John will absorb through her skin. He'll find his way to her bloodstream, and become a permanent part of her.

But now in the dying light Helen looks like a chalky demon as she stares out to sea. The bit of John she dumped in the airport toilet is oozing through soil and sand, and she'd like to think it will eventually season the ocean just steps away from her ashy shins. Helen pulls out a bottle of rum from her tote. A taste for the syrupy stuff is one thing that she's kept from her bacchanalian adventures with Jules. After taking a long intoxicating draw, Helen walks up the beach and finds a comfy nook where she can have her own private hullabaloo.

Before she sits, however, she pats her empty pocket, just to make sure.

Staggerwing

At 6'6" Will Andrews towered above most people, and sometimes his extreme height made him dizzy. It didn't help matters that his fifty-eight-year-old knees were now a touch arthritic. In the Japan Air terminal at Narita International Airport, he had particular trouble finding his stride. He stumbled and righted himself, a tipsy, giant buoy unmoored above a sea of inky heads.

His boss had said his contact would meet him at the baggage carousel.

"Not sure who it will be, but they'll send someone to meet you," Stewart said as they reviewed the final plans for the installation. "Usually it's this guy Tashiro," Stewart continued, "His English sucks, but he seems to understand everything I say."

As head preparator, Stewart usually did the overseas jobs, but he had grown too fat. The Air and Space Museum would have had to pay for two airplane seats, or worse, a first-class ticket to send Stewart to oversee the installation of the loaned Beechcraft C17L Staggerwing at the Tokorozowa Aviation Museum outside of Tokyo. Will, the only other preparator at the museum with enough seniority and engineering skill, was going in his stead.

Now Will scoured the line of men and women waiting by the baggage carousel holding little cards with Western names. Greyson, Kaufmann, Veerhoven, Schmidt. No Andrews. No him. Will worried he had botched the job already. Walked the wrong way. Gone to the wrong baggage claim area.

"Mr. Andrews?"

Will turned. The young woman stood inches away. She was at least a head taller than most of the other Japanese women there picking up luggage or guests. Tall, but not as tall as he.

"Yes?" He said.

"I am so very sorry. I am late and I have no sign." She panted. Will noticed beads of sweat on her upper lip.

"That's okay," Will reassured. "I just got here. There's no problem, no problem at all."

Her brow furrowed for a moment, then relaxed. "I am Mariko Hisheguro, assistant to Tashiro Tasegasei." The woman bowed.

"William Andrews," Will bowed too, and immediately worried it wasn't the right thing to do, returning this gesture. How stupid of him not to study his book on Japanese etiquette. Seventeen hours tucked away in his backpack in overhead storage, its spine uncracked. But the previous 48 hours with his wife Isabelle had worn him out. Her irrational, paranoid mutterings exhausted Will like repetitive jackhammering, not quite abrasive enough to completely unnerve him, but stressful enough to send Will off on this journey with a dull, persistent headache, popping Zantacs like candy.

"Welcome to Japan, Mr. Andrews," Mariko Hisheguro bowed again. Her dark hair fell in two unified sheets by her cheeks.

Will grinned, no bow. I should've read the book, he said to himself. He was usually quite diligent about these kinds of things. Instead Will had watched every movie Japan Air offered, and dozed intermittently in a blissful stupor.

"You had a comfortable journey?" she asked.

"Oh yes. Very comfortable," Will nodded repeatedly, his head an absurdly bouncing ball.

"We will take the tram to your hotel. It is not private like taxi, but it is fast."

"The tram sounds fine," Will said. "I like public transportation." Mariko looked at him oddly. "Unless you want to go by taxi. Really, I'm easy." Now Will was the one sweating.

"I'm sorry," said Mariko. "My English is a problem. I have been told my accent is good, but my comprehension is not so good. What does this mean, 'I'm easy'?"

"Oh, well, um, it means it doesn't matter to me," he shrugged. "That either form of transportation is perfectly acceptable. Tram or taxi, I am happy."

She nodded. "Good. Good."

They stood for a moment, almost eye to eye, so strange for Will, her tallness, and he assumed even stranger for her.

"So, which is it?" Will asked. "Tram or taxi?"

"I think tram." She looked down and away. "It is more appropriate."

Mariko escorted him all the way to the hotel. She insisted on wheeling his suitcase, and walked a few paces ahead of him. Will tried not to look too closely at her gangly and appealing frame from behind. Her outfit was not sexy or stylish. A navy blue blazer and knee-length skirt. Flat black shoes. She's an attractive young woman, he reminded himself, so as not to feel too guilty about this percolation. That's all.

Mariko got the keycard for him from the concierge.

"To open with," she said as she placed the flat plastic sliver in his palm, a solemn offering. She bowed and said goodbye in the lobby, freeing the handle of his suitcase so he could finally grab it and stop feeling so incapable. She managed to communicate that she would pick him up in three hours and take him to the museum, where he would meet the installation crew and oversee the assembly of the Staggerwing. Will bowed—surely this was the right thing to do—and said goodbye in return.

His hotel room was small, clean, and odorless. He didn't check on Isabelle. There was the time change, after all, and some degree of surety with Eleanor, Isabelle's sister, care-taking in his absence. Will didn't unpack his suitcase. He didn't take a nap. Instead he took out Japan-Culture Smart! The Essential Guide to Customs and Culture, sat in the ergonomically pleasing easy chair and read the book from cover to cover.

The car ride with Mariko to the museum later that day afforded a richer exchange, if still awkward.

"So have you lived in Tokyo your whole life?" he asked.

Mariko continued to look out the front window. Traffic was heavy, but orderly. He appreciated her caution. "But for I went to University in Osaka," she answered.

"And what did you study?"

"Engineering."

"Ah." Will wasn't one to believe in signs—he trusted more in quantifiable equations—but this seemed like something to note. And the lurch in his gut told him so. "Me too. Aeronautics."

She nodded and smiled. "We have a thing in comma."

"Do you mean a thing in common?"

Mariko's flat and smooth nose wrinkled around the bridge. "I hope I did not offend." Her pink bottom lip pushed forward.

"No, no. Not offensive at all. Comma is a very benign word." He patted her shoulder, a spontaneous gesture of reassurance. As soon as he did he remembered a particular passage from his guide book:

"Avoid physical contact at all times, such as slapping backs or holding people by the arm while talking, except perhaps during convivial, all-male drinking sessions."

Mariko didn't flinch. She continued the conversation matter-of-factly. "Comma means what?"

So no offense taken, but Will needed to be more cautious. "Comma is the name of the punctuation mark we put in sentences to show a pause." He sounded stodgy. Too cautious, perhaps.

"I'm sorry," she frowned. "I don't understand."

Will cleared his throat hoping to harness a more carefree, youthful tone. "I'll demonstrate." He raised his hand and air wrote, "Mariko is a very good driver comma, one who pays close attention to traffic comma, pedestrians comma, and keeps her eyes on the road period." Commas were indicated with quick downward flicks of the wrist and the period with a dramatic frontward pop of pinched thumb and forefinger.

Mariko tittered at his gestures, like a tiny woodland creature gleeful at finding a stash of unsullied nuts.

Will laughed also, but realizing it had been decades since he'd let go with this sloppy type of belly-deep guffaw, he quickly shut himself up like a vise.

The 45-minute drive out to Tokorozowa Aviation Museum became Will's favorite part of his seven-day stay. It was the only time he and Mariko were alone together. Their conversations thrilled him, and he wasn't sure why. So much of their exchange was based on misunderstanding and backtracked explanation, like a horizontal spiral moving forward, and looping back around on itself before moving forward again. He was not sure if Mariko shared his pleasure with their conversations or the easy space between words. She might just be polite.

On day three, she called him William, not Mr. Andrews, without any prompting on his part. According to the chapter on "The Use of Names" in his etiquette book, "In general, Japanese people will address people by their last name if they are anything but good friends."

They were standing next to each other, gazing up at the partially-assembled brilliant yellow Staggerwing. The body of the plane stood cocked up and forward on its tail and rubber wheel. It looked naked to Will, vulnerable. Like a giant bee stripped of wings. The crew was assembling the plane's double set of wings in another area of the giant Tokorozowa hangar when Mariko touched his arm and said, "William. What is the meaning of Staggerwing?"

Will cleared his throat, and tried to forget the lingering sensation of Mariko's warm hand on his bare forearm. "Well, in aeronautics we refer to 'stagger' as the horizontal positioning of wings in relation to each other when there's more than one set of wings. When the upper wing is positioned behind the lower wing, as is the case with this beauty, we call it negative stagger."

"Negative stagger?" Mariko pronounced each syllable of the words with a halt. They almost sounded Japanese.

"It's not bad," Will shrugged. "It's just a very unsentimental use of engineering terms." He looked back towards workers. He really should have been over there, supervising.

On day four, Mariko invited him to dinner at her home.

"It would be an honor if you would go to my home for dinner this night," she said then added, "Will?"

Will, the shortened version of his name, the most familiar. Or was it just part of the question, as in "Will you come to dinner with me?" Either way, he replied, "I would love to," trying to bridle his joy.

"Very good." Mariko smiled widely, revealing wet teeth and a flash of rosy gums.

"Very, very good!" Will agreed.

"I wait for you," she said as she pulled into the hotel driveway. "Here in car. Do not rush. I am happy."

Upstairs, Will stood in the shower scrubbing, prepping for the evening ahead. His nakedness, an undeniable fact of bathing, now had new associations. Not that he hadn't cared for his body, eaten sensibly, exercised regularly. But the sensation of the soapy washcloth rubbing his hairy arms and legs was almost too much to bear. He avoided his genitals. Just let the water trail down over his penis, washing away any smell, any sweat, any untoward thoughts.

Will hadn't expected the parents. Or the dog, Sobuku, who seemed at first to be the least wary of him. He had assumed dinner at Mariko's would be a pairing, a polite meal, sitting across from each other in what he imagined would be a tiny but neat kitchen in a tiny but neat apartment. But this was a family affair. He removed his shoes and put on the slippers he'd been provided, and followed Mariko's kimono-wearing mother as she shuffled across the wooden floor.

Her parents spoke no English, so over dinner Mariko interpreted their questions.

"How is your work at the Aviation Museum proceeding?"

"What is your city of origin?"

"Is the Japanese cuisine to your liking?"

[167]

Each time Mariko looked at him, Will was sure he detected a special, secret twinkle. He would check his book when he returned to the hotel, but now he asked himself: For a girl like Mariko to introduce him to her parents? Well now, that must have more meaning than he could ever have hoped for.

Will offered appropriate compliments about the food, the Hisheguro home, the wonderful Sobuku. The Hisheguros smiled and laughed. Will felt almost relaxed.

When the questions got more personal, the air became charged in a different way. Chopsticks rested on little ebony platforms. Mariko's perfect eyes averted. Sobuku panted excitedly in the corner.

"Are you married?"

"Where is Mrs. Andrews?"

He answered matter-of-factly, hoped the heat rising from under his collar would not cause him to blush.

After a flustered exchange with her parents Mariko said, "They want to know your intentions."

"Intentions?" He had giddy feelings, that was sure. Desire, yes, particularly when Mariko threw her head back and laughed, her neck swan-like and exposed. But were those intentions?

Mariko frowned. "They wish to know the plan."

"Plan for what?" he whispered. He was sure his cheeks were aflame.

"Plan for the Staggerwing."

Will sighed. Plans were easy, intentions not so. He comfortably described the basic details of installation, how the Staggerwing was the perfect plane to lend. He mentioned how, aside from its historical relevance in the 'Golden Age of Flight,' this bright yellow bird with black stripes, blunt nose, and whirling sliver propeller set speed records and won many races. That a staggered wing arrangement, negative or otherwise, was not only practical but beautiful as well. Something it shared with much Japanese design.

"Take this for example," he said, holding up the deep blue ceramic bowl he had just eaten a delicious noodly concoction from. "Simple, functional and captivating."

There was much head nodding and smiling on the part of the Hisheguros. Everyone seemed pleased.

While exchanging goodbyes at the front door, Mariko's mother suddenly grabbed her daughter's arm and pulled her back towards the kitchen. All Will could make out was Mariko repeating a word which sounded like "Eye, eye," followed by some other Japanese complications. He stood for an uncomfortable moment with Mr. Hisheguro by the front door, both men smiling and nodding, nodding and smiling until the women returned.

Mariko held the freshly washed blue bowl up to him. "A gift to remember us by," she said, the twinkle back in her eye. "We hope it will find good use in your wife's kitchen."

Back in his hotel room Will Google-searched Japanese phonetics for words sounding like "eye" with only his American ears to guide him. After reconfiguring A's and I's and E's, he settled on "Ai" and a link to "Japanese Terms of Endearment" gave him:

"Ai（愛）" can be roughly translated as 'love' in English."

Lurching stomach. Beating heart. A bowl, a lovely girl, a two-letter word. The question of intention swirling among other thoughts in his brain, a flower among twigs stuck in a whirlpool.

For the remaining days, Mariko watched Will intently from the sidelines while he worked with the installation crew at Tokorozowa. Their conversations no longer felt quite so circuitous. There was still much confusion, on Will's part, at least. But Mariko's words felt unleashed. Like Will's desktop toy, his Newton's Cradle. Metal balls hanging inert until the end ball soared outward and starting a noisy volley with a satisfying smack.

The Staggerwing assembly proceeded with remarkable precision. Will powered in full command, fueled by Mariko's presence, thrilled when her creature-like giggles rose above the drone of screw guns and chop saws. While driving, she rested her free hand on his shoulder, laughing at his jokes and unintentional faux pas. She lingered in hellos and goodbyes. On their final night together she became confessional over sake at the hotel bar. There was a boyfriend whom she no longer loved, who had betrayed her and broken her heart.

"Kobayashi is a bad man," she said. "It takes me a long while to forget him."

Will reached over and patted the top of her warm, white hand. "Poor Mariko," he said.

She looked at him with a steady eye-to-eye gaze. "No worry, William. I am fine now. I am ready for love again."

+++++++

Once he was back in the states, Will began revealing himself to Mariko through emails sent from a secret account. He only sent them from his iPhone, and only when he could steal time away from Isabelle. He wrote about his lonely childhood. His allergy to cats. His fallen arches. His inability to hold a tune. He lamented his failed ambition, never working as a real aeronautics engineer and settling instead for the job at the Air and Space Museum. How he was sick of restoring old planes and designing the exhibitions those old planes resided in. He told her about Isabelle's mental instability, the decades of shifting diagnoses. The long line of fired shrinks. He told her about their recent move to a farmhouse. A place he'd hoped would provide Isabelle

[171]

with peace and a sense of purpose. He told Mariko he wanted to escape.

One afternoon, three weeks in to farm life and barely settled, the weather conspired in Will's favor. He was grateful for the dismal wetness, the heavy air, the impossibility of outdoor chores. Isabelle would be docile, easily placated. Rain did that to her. If Will's luck held, she would wander around the new house grazing cold fingers on bannisters, across countertops, calling out reminders, "Lovey, let's not forget the green paint," or seeking opinions, "Lovey, what do you think we should do about that broken window sash?"

Historically, sunny days were his enemies and rainy days his friends. Isabelle was a hothouse flower when the sun shone, a crazy hybrid rose. Will's every word caught in her twisted prickly vines, providing food for Isabelle's misguided thoughts and thorny miscalculations.

He had just sent one of his gushy emails to Mariko. A wash of guilt would likely soak him later that day, the way it did whenever he sent these secret missives. For now, Will stared out the door of his newly purchased, structurally decrepit barn and felt relieved.

But hopes for a peaceful day were dashed when Isabelle raced in through the open barn door with blood pouring from her right hand.

"What happened?" he asked. The iPhone slipped easily into the back pocket of his overalls.

"I was washing a bowl and it shattered," she wailed.

"Oh Bunny Belle, I'm so sorry," He stood with his hands turned outward.

Isabelle was tiny. The top of her greying, blonde-haired head barely even with Will's solar plexus. She thrust her bloody palm under his nose. The metallic odor made him shiver. He grasped her wrist and held the hand further away so he could examine the damage. There were three deep cuts across her palm.

"It just crumbled in my hands. Cut me, goddamn it," Isabelle snarled. "I hate blood, you know I hate blood, Will."

An ancient claim, yet Isabelle had purposely cut herself numerous times in the past. Never on her palms though. Always discreetly; the hidden folds of inner thighs, the soft white insides of upper arms.

"I think we should have a doctor look at this," Will sighed. "You may need stitches."

Isabelle howled. Incoherent, inconsolable.

He could feel her pulse under his thumb. The blood in her wounds was clotting, but with any sudden moves it would ooze again. He tightened his grip in case she started to flail. With his other hand he stroked her hair, and when she was less tremulous he leaned towards her. "Poor Bunny," he cooed. "I know, I know."

He calculated risks, estimated travel times, imagined and located car keys, wallets, eyeglasses. All this while covering Isabelle's blotched tear-salted cheeks with gentle asexual kisses, slowly walking her towards the car, raising her bloody hand higher, above both their hearts.

Post-emergency room visit, Isabelle had once again, stopped paying attention and dropped her bandaged hand into her lap. She slumped forward against the seat belt, forgetting to keep her mutilated palm elevated.

"Keep it upright Bunny," Will said gently, "Otherwise it wont stop bleeding."

"Sorry," she sighed, weakly lifting her forearm. She'd been relentlessly apologetic the entire drive to the hospital, a shivering nervous wreck pacing the ER, and an angry, irrational non-complier in the exam room. Now she was docile. Dull.

"No need to apologize Bunny. We'll be home in ten minutes." Will told himself to be patient. Isabelle had had a trauma after all, a legitimate accident. "I'll make you a nice nest of pillows, and a bolster as a bridge for that arm."

"Always engineering," her words slurred, the sedatives having a last hurrah in her bloodstream. "So things work out for me."

"Yes," he sighed. "That's my job."

"I'm sorry I broke the bowl, Lovey. Such a gorgeous blue. You brought it all the way from Japan. Just for me."

He coughed, trying to hide the catch in his breath.

"Irreplaceable?" Isabelle whispered.

"No Bunny," Will lied profoundly.

"I think it was defective," Isabelle declared, also a lie. But loud and clear as a bell.

The destruction of Mariko's bowl caused a different kind of lurch in his stomach, the desire to howl himself. Ai, he thought, repeating the word over and over in his mind. Ai, Ai, Ai.

When they got home, he settled Isabelle in bed with the promised bolster, covered her up, and kissed her on the forehead like a loving parent. Isabelle fell asleep instantly, her eyes restless under closed lids, her lips parted slightly, a tiny sour breath escaping with each sigh. Will left her and went down to the kitchen.

The indigo blue bowl was in shards, scattered at the bottom of the sink in a shallow pool of slimy dishwater. She must have thrown it. Will picked each piece out and placed it on the counter. He held them all, lining up the sharp edges, trying to put the bowl back together, but there were too many gaps, too many small slivers missing.

While Will always deleted his gushing emails to Mariko as soon as he sent them, he couldn't bring himself to erase the ones she sent back. He loved deciphering her phonetically awkward spelling. In June he learned of a childhood friend named Joji, who either lived or had lived in St. Louis. He wasn't sure which. In July, he learned of Mariko's desire to see the Grand Canyon and eat an American hot dog, though not necessarily at the same time. Or maybe that was what she wanted: to eat an American hot dog while staring down that beautiful American abyss. In August, she was very happy, because Joji-chan had returned to Tokyo. Or was returning.

He was certain each note from Mariko held a clue. Will poured over her sweet, stilted missives in the darkness of the barn, squinting at the screen of his smartphone, paying extra close attention to her sign offs:

Your words fill me with hope and joy.

We are both ready for love.

I await your return with impatience.

"Can't Stewart go this time?" Isabelle moaned, sinking to the kitchen floor, her skirt pooled around her like brown sugar.

"He can't, Bunny Belle," Will said, trying to sound disappointed. "He hasn't lost any weight in the three months the Staggerwing's been on loan."

"I could come with you." Will could see out of the corner of his eye that Isabelle had both hands in her lap, the right one clawing the palm of the left, where red welts reminded them both of the broken bowl.

"Don't rub like that," He turned to face her, his own hands covered in sloppy suds. "The skin is still recovering."

Isabelle dropped her hands to her sides. She gazed up at Will from the wide planked wood floor, her eyes wild and wet. Barely focused. Quivering in their sockets.

"That's okay. I know it's hard for you," he said.

"It's all hard. Everything. All of it."

"I know, I know."

"I don't think I can stand it. You leaving again."

"It will be fine. You love this place, right?"

"I love it with you here with me. I don't know if I love it without you. I don't think I can do it."

Will wanted to sink to the floor himself. All nobility and good-natured care-taking was gone. He could leave Isabelle. He would make this second trip to Japan, see Mariko. He would supervise the de-installation of the Staggerwing, something he could do in his sleep. It was easier to take things apart than to put them back together.

Will left Isabelle, again with her sister, and a new prescription.

+++++++

He got off the plane at Narita and found not only Mariko waiting for him, but her parents as well.

The Hisheguros greeted him with smiles and bows.

"We are all so happy you have returned," Mariko told him. "My parents want you to share in their recent joy."

"Okay," Will said, overwhelmed that he could share anything approaching joy with the Hisheguro's.

"I have told them of our communications," she said. "They know of our connection."

Will couldn't speak, so filled with joy himself. Maybe intentions were possible after all.

They piled into Mariko's car, the elder Hisheguros insisting on the back seat, joking that "the two tall ones should have the honor of the front." There was much animated chatter in the car, but not any Will could understand. Mariko looked over at him, and with a hand on his shoulder—in front of her parents no less—she said, "I have a special surprise for you. We will go to my home for you to see."

When they pulled up to the Hisheguros, there was a young man standing outside waiting for them. He ran to open the car door for Will.

"Mr. Andrews," he bowed.

Mr. Hisheguro slapped Will's back good-naturedly from the back seat, demanding him to get out, get out! As soon as Will did so the young stranger held out his hand. In impeccable English he said, "I'm Joji Kobayashi, Mariko's fiancé. I'm totally stoked to finally meet you."

Dinner at the Hisheguros was excruciating. Will was polite as ever, but he drank too much sake while listening without comment to Joji-chan babble on about his time in St. Louis at Washington University, his love of hot dogs and the Grand Canyon, that "Awesome American Wonder of the World."

Will returned to his hotel room alone, with a splitting headache brewing. He sat in the ergonomically correct chair, annoyed now by how seductively comfortable and well-designed it was. He reviewed Mariko's emails on his laptop with Google open, and Japan-Culture Smart! at his side, ready to probe even deeper.

"Chan. An endearment added to the end of a first name."

"Joji-chan. A lover, not a friend."

"Ai. With different kanji characters, <u>ai</u> (藍) means 'indigo blue.'"

Ai. Not love, just color.

For Will, the loveless color of a hospitable gift.

Will could only dig so far. He erased all of Mariko's emails, every trace.

Will dismantled the Staggerwing in two days, working round the clock side-by-side with the Tokowozowa crew, adding solo shifts, declining daily dinner invitations from the Hisheguros, claiming false deadlines and pressures. Mariko brought 'Joji-chan' to the museum to watch Will work, so proud of her American friend. Will avoided them as best he could, and worked hard to mask his private humiliation. He felt like a caged gorilla in a zoo, a simpleminded creature whose cluelessness landed him in the most woeful of circumstances.

+++++++

"Three days early! You couldn't bear to be gone from us," Isabelle joked. "Me and my crazies."

Will smoothed a loose curl behind her ear.

"Eleanor wasn't too bad this time. You'll be glad to know she got me to do a bit of yoga. I think it might be good for me, all that spiritual mumbo-jumbo."

He nodded.

"It's good to be back where you belong, isn't it?"

He nodded again.

"Lovey, you're so quiet. Are you feeling okay?" Isabelle reached high to place a dry cracked palm on his forehead. "You are a tad warm."

"It's just jet-lag. Such a quick back and forth. Hard on this old man's system."

"I'll make us some supper. After some good home cooking you'll be right as rain." Isabelle's full function mode might last a week, a month, two months.

Dishes done, sweet kisses laid on married cheeks, Isabelle went up to bed. Will wandered around his house with the fresh eyes of the newly jaded. His thirst was insatiable. He lurched towards the kitchen. While drinking from the kitchen faucet, Will stepped on something sharp. It was a small stab, a splinter, a surprise. Will hobbled over to the couch and turned on the overhead light. He plucked the splinter out of his foot and saw it wasn't a splinter after all. It was a shard, a sliver of blue. Indigo. Ai.

Bigfoot

Mae looked around the table at the other moms and tried not to be too obviously observational. She sipped her kombucha, wishing it were a Coke, the real sugary poisoned brew. The cola crack she slugged down in the good old days when she worked at Morgan Stanley around the clock protecting corporate client investments. Kombucha tasted the way Mae imagined pulverized crab grass soaked in goat piss might taste. But the other moms swore by it, so Mae kept her mouth shut and sucked the stuff through a soggy paper straw.

Things had begun innocently a few months earlier, with an invitation from Keisha to come sit at their table at Playce, a neighborhood cafe/playroom/bar that featured rubberized flooring, booze and a communal stash of unhygienic toys. Keisha's three year old daughter Saskia was the 'It Girl' of Playce. Most mornings Saskia held court on the squooshy Playce floor, with other toddlers lying at her feet while she sat regal and cross-legged, gesticulating like a shaman. When Saskia wasn't holding court, she and Mae's daughter Cassie were inseparable. The two little girls hugged each other and skipped around Playce calling themselves 'The Two Headed Kid.' Perverse and adorable.

It was a social coup, this toddler bonding, important to Mae because Keisha also reigned at Playce, along with her mom-friends Abby and Sarah. For some unfathomable reason, this unassuming trio in saggy sweaters and fleece-lined clog boots had power. Mommy Power. Even with extra pounds around their midriffs, bad hair, and sleep-deprived raccoon eyes. Everyone loved these schlumpy moms, or ached to be them.

Mae secretly called them the Imperfects. And she wanted in.

Mae was an unabashed power junkie, accustomed to being at the top of every heap. But she had lost footing recently. She'd been let go from her high-level finance job. Climbing the ladder and clocking the hours had been easy breezy at first. Then, bye bye Mae-Mae. Her entire department was obliterated with no warning, but gobs of severance. Not that she needed the money. Money had been one thing she had never needed to scramble for. Lucky Mae.

Still, life was suddenly like bungee-jumping without any rebound.

Splat.

Keisha's invitation to sit at the Imperfects' table was a way back up, an easy ascent, or so Mae assumed. She bought the requisite oversized sexless sweater. The clogs were less comfortable; her toes jammed up against the fluffy fronts like blind moles searching for air. Never one to give up, Mae endured the pain.

How hard could being a perfect Imperfect be? Talk about an uphill battle. So far everything Mae had done or said was shrugged off by the reigning triumverate, or worse, ignored. And now there were these disturbing moments when Mae's renegade inner voice blew all over the place, like a dirty plastic shopping bag skittering down the sidewalk.

Goat piss. Pulverized crab grass. Brains like jello at the bottom of the abyss.

Such weirdness percolating in Mae's brain. As she worked hard to keep her nasty inner monologue at bay, Abby, Queen of the Imperfects, exploded through the Playce doorway, pushing her stroller like a first responder with a battering ram. Her coat was open despite the freezing outside chill. Damp sweat glistened on Abby's chest, droplets trickling down cleavage between giant still-nursing boobs. Her hair was Brillo-ed. Her cheeks were flushed. Her eyes were buggy.

Mae observed Abby morph into a giant bee. The Queen Bee, with antennae, jittery wings and scrambly little twisted legs.

"I'm finally fucking here!" Abby cried.

Mae shook her head tic-like, and Abby became Abby again.

A pod of boring moms at another table stared at the Queen with parted lips and droopy lovesick eyes. Mae imagined the Un-Cools hoarding Imperfect swag, swiping Abby's used napkins, making shrines out of Sarah's lipstick-smeared coffee cups, surreptitiously snipping off tips of Keisha's dreads. Maybe Mae should beat them to the chase.

Grab, grab, grab. Mine, mine, mine.

"Abby. Girl, you look like shit," laughed Keisha with hee-haw chuckles, endearing to the other Imperfects.

"I know." Abby plopped her lumpy body on the end of the bench and pointed at her son in his stroller. "Another shower-less morning, thanks to my evil spawn."

Evil spawn, thought Mae? Abby's adorable rapscallion Dash charmed the pants off everyone and would no doubt keep his future wife in a constant frenzy of excitement and hot panic. Plus, said evil spawn now slept like a ginger angel in his stroller.

"I'm ready to sign him up now for military boarding school. I swear." Abby groaned.

Here was Mae's chance to be witty, ironic. Get kudos from the Queen. Mae offered a crisp salute. "It did wonders for me," she chirped.

Abby stared blankly. "You went to military boarding school? Like, for real?"

Mae guffawed, nowhere near as charmingly as Keisha. "No. I was joking."

Abby stared at Mae for a blank, unreadable second, then turned away to fumble with the safety straps of Dash's stroller. "Let's air this sucker out."

Goat Piss. Pulverized crab grass. Frizzy-headed Queen bees. A failed, flat joke.

With Abby's arrival, the Imperfects could hunker down and do what they liked to do best. They kvetched. While their children ran amok knocking into each other, grabbing toys that didn't belong to them, pooping in diapers that remained unchanged until smells overwhelmed, the Imperfects shared irksome details of their lives because, hey, they were all just a tad frustrated.

Keisha's surgeon husband snored and had gained 30 pounds since Saskia was born. Sarah was responsible for her Asperger's-ish pain-in-the-ass sister now that their parents had fled to Florida full time. Abby was considering anti-anxiety meds because she totally freaked every time her husband, a semi-famous screenwriter, flew to LA.

Mae shifted her position, trying to get her butt comfortable on the hardwood bench. She didn't know how to kvetch. Besides, what could she complain about? Perfect teeth? Her thick and lustrous product-free waist-length blonde hair? Her tranquil toddler Cassie speaking in full sentences and sleeping through the night? Her husband Julian, with his charming British accent and successful tech business, still incredibly generous, still attentively great in bed? Her unwavering ability to add long columns of six-digit figures in her head, even though she hadn't had any reason to do so since leaving her publically shamed finance group, herself scandal-free? That Cassie was born vaginally after only five hours of labor? That in spite of her perfect body, Mae barely exercised, and when she did work out she was mistaken for a fitness instructor, or a professional athlete? Would the Imperfects, or anyone else for that matter, believe Mae if she griped that here, at Playce morning meet-ups, being just plain Perfect was a burden?

Maybe she should lift her tee-shirt right now and show off those washboard abs. Mae fiddled with her hem.

Just then Sydney, Playce's premier barista, approached the Imperfects' table. Transgender Sydney reminded Mae of a pumped up Dennis the Menace; life sized, with a slight hint of boobage. Mae could never remember if Sydney was a FTM or a MTF. She sensed that asking for clarification would be a blatant faux pas.

"How're you lovely ladies doing?" asked Sydney.

Mae looked up at Sydney and attempted a kvetch. "I have really big feet."

It was true. Mae's feet were massive, her toes themselves almost as long as her daughter's fingers.

There was a confused beat before Sydney smiled at Mae. But it was forced; a rigor mortis grin Sydney reserved for Playce customers who annoyed or made entitled demands. A grimace quite unlike the golden friendship-oozing smile Sydney now bestowed on the Imperfects.

"So, what can I get my favorite mamas?" Sydney asked.

"I'll take a latte, Syd," Abby drawled.

"Another kombucha, darling," said Keisha.

"Jasmine tea, if you guys still have the organic," Sarah nodded.

Mae wanted coffee. Just regular coffee. But Sydney turned away, leaving Mae caffeine-free and dangling at the end of the bench like a decorative tassel.

+++++++

When Mae was eight years old she got sick from eating too fast at the Plantation Winds Country Club pool. The culprit was a frankfurter, gulped in three bites, washed further down her gullet by bubbly orange pop. Immediately afterwards, Mae jumped in the pool to play underwater tea party with Sandy Bradford. Mae felt her stomach knot while hovering near the bottom of the pool, miming sips with pinky raised and head nodding like a Victorian Englishwoman. When she and Sandy came up for air, Mae ignored the queasiness creeping from her belly to her thorax.

"Let's do it again!" shouted Sandy, an endless fount of energy and enthusiasm whom Mae secretly found annoying. But Sandy Bradford had social cachet with the underage set at Plantation Winds. And if Sandy wanted to play tea party, then hell yeah, Mae was gonna play tea party till she was blue in the face, or green to the gills. Which Mae was. Both green and blue, before she threw up underwater in a spreading brownish ooze.

A shrill and humiliating whistle was blown by Chet, the lifeguard. The Plantation Winds Pool was closed for the rest of the afternoon. All the nannies, mothers, and children packed up their gear and headed to the air conditioned clubhouse for ping pong, TV, mint juleps. All except Mae and her mother. They made the hastiest of exits.

Mama burned rubber out of the parking lot. The car was stifling, the air conditioning wouldn't kick in until they were halfway home. Still Mae was covered in goosebumps. She clutched the arm rest, felt the seatbelt across her chest like a straight jacket. Her bathing suit was still damp, her bum a bit squishy against the leather seat of the Cadillac.

The car reeked of Coppertone and sweaty rage. Mama's eyes were steely behind her Jackie Os; her tan cheeks twitching as if she had a bunch of marbles inside her clamped mouth and she couldn't decide whether to spit or swallow. Mama's silence lasted the whole ride, like a rubber band stretched to the point of snapping.

For years after the shameful Plantation Winds incident, Mae feared a repetition. Not of vomiting, but of her mother's disappointment. To be shut out by Mama was a gut punch. Mae's earliest, most noxious concern.

Mae lucked out. She grew more and more beautiful, and seemed blessed with a superior intellect. She made all the right friends, got the best grades and the best jobs. Mae never had to endure that silent punishment again. Mama didn't need to prod Mae up to the top of any heaps. Mae hiked them, effortlessly and gladly, on her own.

Everything was hunky dory until Mae's clumsy attempts at Imperfection. Missteps that were accumulating like more upchucked hot dogs, polluting an otherwise perfect record.

+++++++

"Screw this," Mae cried that evening, as she collapsed on the couch next to Julian. "I can't be a plain yellow pumpkin."

"Huh?" Julian looked up from the screen of his iPad. Cassie was asleep; as usual, she'd drifted off after kisses and one lullaby. Never any whining or grasping for more, more, more from that even-keeled secure little girl.

"I will always be a golden carriage." Mae moaned.

"I have no idea what you're talking about," Julian returned to swiping and scrolling and tapping. "But being a transportation vehicle made from a precious metal sounds infinitely superior to life as a boring vegetable."

Julian would never get it. Raised in England. All male boarding schools from the age of eight. No real exposure to the weird world of female friendship. Lucky Prince Charming.

[191]

"Forget it," Mae sighed. She stretched her legs out along the couch, pushing her feet against the side of Julian's thigh.

"Hey," he said. "Watch it, Bigfoot."

May looked across at her reddened toes, her chipped blue nail polish. Her aborted kvetch about her giant dogs earlier that day at the Imperfects' table had resulted in more blank stares and empty pauses. And no free coffee from Syd, a real slap in the face. But what had Mae expected? Complaining about her big feet when the rest of her looked the way it did was like complaining that the spare room on the top floor of her renovated brownstone could use a fresh paint job.

In bed later that night, Mae lay awake, her brain churning. She replayed conversations held at the Imperfects' table earlier that day, interjecting witticisms she hadn't thought of in real life, imagining Abby, in particular, smiling and laughing at her every word.

She looked over at Julian, sleeping peacefully: her benign Brit, quiet as a mouse. She wished he snored like Keisha's overweight husband. Couldn't Julian at least produce some masculine body odor? Collect crumbs in his closely cropped beard?

Maybe Cassie could develop night terrors. Have a tantrum every now and then.

Spread cocksakie. Pink eye. Head lice. Strep.

But no. Mae's perfect family was useless. Plastic pins from the game of Life, two pink, one blue, driving their car round and round, buying all the right properties, choosing all the best professions, but taking all the wrong turns away from Imperfection.

+++++++

The winter weeks rolled by, an endless cycle of naps, princess make-believe games, missing Legos, monotony, and runny noses. The only punctuations were the trips to Playce, where Mae began to feel so inconsequential, it was as if she were melting into an amber puddle by the side of the table.

One frozen day, Sarah came up with an idea. A field trip to TofuTots, a place that ran 'Junior Vegan Chef Workshops' in a trendy (but still dicey) corner of the city. A neighborhood where young restless artistic types lived. An area the Imperfects would only think to visit during daytime hours. A slum, really.

"For fifty dollars each they get to make buckwheat shortbread, coconut oil toffee, and kale chips," Sarah said in her monotone voice. Sarah was a vegan foodie. She provided the Imperfects with all sorts of dry, barely edible snacks. Organic. Gluten-free. Taste-free. Sarah didn't talk much. Mostly she communicated through imperious glares and loaded sighs. When she deigned to speak, the other Imperfects sat upright and listened. She had straight dark hair hanging like an iron curtain to her chin, blunt bangs grazing her arched eyebrows. She never smiled.

[193]

A flapper. A cyborg. A cyborg flapper. A sullen cyborg flapper.

Mae imagined Sarah rising from the table, arms herky jerky, elbows akimbo. Her fingers did little sparkly maneuvers; her knees knocked and her legs scissored. Sarah's face was a mask of disdain, her frown as deep as a Kabuki warrior's.

Ugly. Scary ugly. Sarah Slasher. Haberdasher.

Mae squeezed her eyes shut. She could feel crow's feet scratching at the edges of her lids.

"And for an extra ten bucks, they'll do a puppet show about organic farming," Sarah droned on.

Mae opened her eyes. Sarah was sitting. She had never danced.

"Saskia doesn't do puppet shows," said Keisha. "They freak her out."

"Whatever," sighed Sarah.

Abby stretched her arms overhead and yawned. She'd kvetched earlier: A rough night with Dash while screenwriting hubby was off in Cali pitching a script to the Weinsteins. "I'm cool with anything, but maybe we can skip the toffee. The last thing I want to do is clean that shit out of Dash's hair. Otherwise, awesome idea, Sare."

"Awesome sauce idea!" blurted Mae. She'd overheard this exclamatory adding of 'sauce' recently. Albeit the exclaimer was a prepubescent actress on TV selling smartphones.

The Imperfects glanced at Mae as if she were a slight, inconsequential breeze.

"Isn't that what the kids will cook?" Mae plunged against the tide, against her better judgement. "Awesome sauce? Magic marinara? Holy-shit hollandaise?" Mae's bleating hurt her own ears.

"Um, ah, I don't think so." Sarah said in a sober, conversation-ending tone.

Mae half-heartedly sucked down another punishing kombucha. She felt everything but her merest outline fade away.

+++++++

Mae was alone in the house, listening to Courtney jabber away on the phone. Courtney was Mae's only remaining friend from her Kappa days at Duke. Courtney, southern to the core, was a doctor. A radiologist.

"Why do you hang out with those gals anyway?" asked Courtney, totally non-medically.

Crumbs were flying from Mae's mouth as she made her way through a bag of Chips Ahoy. She'd had a brainstorm at 4 a.m. If she binged regularly she might put on a few pounds and pad that perfect belly of hers. Get a nice mommy pooch going. Earlier in her conversation with Courtney, when her mouth had been empty, Mae had mentioned the upcoming trip to Tofu Tots.

"Everyone loves them." Mae paused before stuffing a twentieth cookie in her mouth. She examined the list of ingredients on the side of the bag. Lots of dangerous, highly-caloric ingestibles.

"Yeah," drawled Courtney, "Everyone but you."

"I love them like Sandy Bradford," Mae sighed.

"Who?" asked Courtney.

"No one. Forget it."

Courtney was quiet. In the background Mae could hear riffs of 'Fur Elise' being played not-too-shabbily by one of Courtney's unquestionably talented daughters.

Finally Courtney spoke. "I think you've landed in the wrong circle, Mae-Mae. You need to be adored. All those young bucks at Morgan Stanley? I remember when I visited you there, before Adelaide was born. Those guys would've licked your big-ass platypus feet if you'd asked them."

"Aha!" Mae cried. "See? What you just did there?"

"What?" Courtney asked.

"You jabbed me about my feet."

"Oh, I'm sorry," Courtney lied.

"These 'gals' as you call them, they don't do that. They don't jab. They don't snark. They're, like, perfect. Perfectly Imperfect."

"Well they sound boring as all git out to me. And that trip ya'all are taking to, what again? A vegetarian cooking school?"

"Vegan. Not vegetarian." Mae corrected.

"Whatever. All vegetables. That sounds like the ultimate snooze." Courtney paused and called away from her phone: "That's wonderful, Addie! You've done Ludwig Von proud!"

Mae stared out the living room window just as Julian and Cassie cruised up to the stoop, each on a scooter, Cassie wearing helmet, wrist guards, and knee pads. Mae watched Julian lovingly remove Cassie's protective armor. Other dads hurled their kids around caveman-style, urged them to run ahead on sidewalks, took them to cafes in their footsie pajamas with hair and teeth unbrushed. They were men who gladly handed over their smartphones in exchange for some peace and quiet. At the very least, some dads let their kids go hatless and gloveless on winter days. Julian did none of those things. Mae was doomed.

+++++++

Once again that night, Mae was ragged and wide awake while Julian lay beside her in an enviable, oblivious stupor. At 2 a.m. she got out of bed to look at herself in the bathroom mirror to see if maybe, hopefully, she looked as shitty as she felt.

Sleep-deprived and cookie-poisoned, hair mussed and face purposely unwashed, Mae still looked gorgeous, even in the glare of the fluorescent overheads.

She shuffled out of the bathroom and tiptoed instinctively and maternally past Cassie's door. Mae didn't want to wake her baby up.

Or, hey, maybe she did. A cranky kid at TofuTots might provide a kvetch-worthy step towards Imperfection.

Mae approached Cassie's toddler-sized canopy bed, a bed to adore, an overstuffed overflowing fluffy fest of rosy duvets and frilly euro shams. Mae stared down at her perfect slumbering child.

"Cassie," cooed Mae. "Oh Cahhhseee."

Cassie was down for the count, a charming pool of drool next to her plump little lips on the pink flannel pillow case.

Mae's own mother had never woken her up like this, not with such bad, selfish motives. Really, it was no better than a kidnapper coming through a window in the dead of night! But then again, Mama never woke Mae up at all. Not for school in the morning, or church on Sundays. Mama had been an early adopter of Jazzercise. She took morning classes religiously, bounding back home afterward in puce and magenta spandex, a few stray blonde hairs clinging to her flushed and dewy forehead. Mama was energized and chatty. Nicer, in fact, than she would be later in the day, when the mundane aspects of domestic life pulled her back down like heavy stones chained to her slender ankles.

Now Grown-up Mae was desperate, weighted in a different way. She reached down and rattled her own daughter as if she were testing a lightbulb, waiting to hear that tell-tale, tinny broken sound. Cassie stirred, her eyes opened, googly and dazed.

"Hi Cassie-doodle," Mae chirped. "Wanna play?"

Cassie stared at Mae, zombie-blank. She wasn't awake. She was off in Dreamland. Just as Mae realized it, Cassie's eyes closed again.

"Damn it," hissed Mae, clawing her head, plucking out hairs that belonged on a shampoo commercial. As Mae plodded out of Cassie's room, she ripped out a nice little tangle.

+++++++

The next day, the Imperfects boarded the subway, bound for TofuTots.

Saskia and Cassie sat angelically across from Mae, little feet straight out and hands linked, gabbing like a couple of old ladies on a park bench. Abby's Dash and Sarah's Jake slipped and slid all over the seats like a couple of plastered sailors during Fleet Week. Abby and Sarah were deep in an intimate kvetch. Keisha sat next to Mae playing Candy Crush, admirably self-contained. Mae got out her own phone and poked at it, trying to look busy. She scrolled through her photo albums, and came across snaps from her honeymoon in Tahiti, a blissful trip that now seemed as if it had occurred in another lifetime on another planet. To another Mae.

One photo in particular shouted to be shared, and in a fit of desperation Mae thrust her phone under Keisha's nose.

[199]

"Think the vegans will put me in jail if I show them this?" Mae asked. A pig roast. A corral of chubby grass-skirted Tahitian men. Mae stood in the center, string bikinied, an orchid lei draped around her bronzed neck, wielding a spear pointed sadistically at the sizzling pig's rump.

Kiesha stared blandly at the image.

Mae went on. "I'll whip it out and holler: 'Take a look, soybean suckas!'" Now that, that was good, she thought. Really good.

Keisha finally looked up at Mae, her eyes treacly with pity. "That's harsh, girl." she shook her head and frowned. "Like, really harsh." Keisha resumed her masterful crushing of candies.

Fuck, fuck, fail. The check is in the mail.

Mae scratched her head. She plucked a hair. She stared at ads for storage space across the train car, herself crashing and crushed.

+++++++

TofuTots was housed in a decrepit-looking warehouse, the kind of place associated with 1990's cop shows.

Stolen goods. Decomposing bodies. Tofu Tots. Kannibal Kids.

But inside, the former industrial space had been scrubbed clean and spruced up. TofuTots was sanitized, eco-style. Mae resisted the urge to bend down and lick the gleaming floor.

[200]

"Hey, I'm Gus," said the squeaky clean (but not clean-cut) twentysomething who greeted them at the door. Mae thought Gus could strut his stuff down a J.Crew catwalk, if only he got rid of the swirling mass of indecipherable hieroglyphs running up and down his arms, shaved off his weird little goatee, and surgically repaired earlobes that had been stretched circularly with what looked to Mae like Nutter Butter lids.

The toddlers had gathered in a restless, rumbling group. "Are you guys ready to cook up some yummy treats?" Gus gushed.

"I'm ready to eat you, Gus," Abby stage-whispered saucily to the other moms.

Keisha belly-laughed, luscious and adorable. Sarah poked Abby affectionately in Abby's pudgy ribs.

Mae stood off to the side, pawing her hair. She had gathered a few more palm-sized tumbleweeds to stash in the pocket of her jeans.

"Okay then," Gus sang-said. "Come with me little dudes, come with me!" He skipped away, deflating his hipster aura with big dorky strides. The kids followed.

"Angling for some kind of tip, Gussie?" Mae snarled as the Imperfects ran past her to catch up with the scampering boy-man and toddlers.

"What did you say?" Abby asked as she huffed and puffed through a klutzy jog.

"Mr. Tats," Mae answered, as she too started running.

Lemmings, all of us. Scurrying to the edge of a cliff.

"The Pied Piper of bean curd," Mae continued as the Imperfects slowed their pace. She jerked her chin towards Gus. "No doubt he wants us to slip some twenties down his organic cotton briefs once this show is over."

"Um, hello?" Sarah piped in. "Gustav Streller is like, a renowned vegan chef. He owns Pear & Chestnut. You know, the new place down by the waterfront."

"The Ken Doll's name is Gustav?" Mae asked. The neck of her schlumpy wool sweater was too itchy. She tugged at it, stretched it so it hung around her neck like loose elephant skin.

"Yes. Gustav." Cyborg Sarah smirked.

"Wienerschnitzely name for a vegan vunderkind, yah?" Mae said faux-Germanically.

All three Imperfects scowled at Mae, whose hands migrated from the distended collar back to her scalp. She plucked some nice little tufts, swirled little strands.

"Mae. What the fuck are you doing to your hair?" asked Keisha.

Mae dropped her hand and pocketed another blonde mess.

+++++++

Gus corralled the kids by a giant vat at the far end of the cavernous TofuTots. In spite of Abby's protest, they were going to make toffee after all.

[202]

"Moms," called Gus, "If you could all grab caps and smocks for your kids, and the same for yourselves, that would be super." He pointed to an array of green sacks clipped to a line with old timey clothes pins.

Once everyone was TofuTots smocked, and all hair was tucked under TofuTots caps, Gus led them to slop sinks to wash their hands. There were no towels.

"Now shake, shake, shake," cried Gus as he waved his manly paws around in the air, demonstrating the TofuTots approach to hand drying.

The kids went apeshit spraying droplets of water on each other. The Imperfects shook their hands too, abiding by Master Gustav's instructions. Mae tried her best, but she was weary. So, so weary. Her hands wouldn't dry. They were wet, and cold too, so she put them behind her back and wiped the remains on the rear of her smock.

"Cassie's mommy did a no-no," whined Jake, pointing at Mae. "She wiped her hands on her tushy."

No one seemed to notice. No one seemed to care. They all skedaddled away from Mae, over to the toffee vat, where Gus handed out large wooden spoons and bags of brown sugar. Mae staggered towards them. Cassie had already found her place on her own, atop a wooden step stool. Part of the gang. Mae came to stand beside her.

"Having fun, Sweet Pea?" Mae asked in a strained and high pitched voice.

Cassie looked up at her mother, perplexed, with an expression that said Who are you, anyway? Then Cassie turned back to the vat, while Gus instructed all the kids to pour, pour, pour their bags of brown sugar into the muddy pool.

Mae had no bag. She had no spoon. She'd been left out of the distribution. She looked around at the expectant faces of the kids and the smirky, contented faces of the Imperfects. Her own woozy swirl, her ragged edges, her spent psyche, punched her drunk.

The others dipped their spoons, stirring.

A cabal of witches. Murder. Mayhem.

There was no winning. No winning at all. Mae stared down at the gloppy toffee mass. She inhaled the sickly sweet fumes: brown sugar, vegan butter replacement, toddler glee, maternal joy. She was overwhelmed with desire.

Other ways to win, Mae-Mae. More than one way to skin a cat.

The TofuTots smock and shower cap came off first. Then Mae released her feet from the sweaty toe-pinching fleece-lined clogs and pulled the schlumpy sweater over her head. Off came her jeans. She stepped out of her thong, unsnapped her bra, released her pert stretch-mark-free breasts.

Use it, don't abuse it.

Mae's big feet went in first. Her long toes slathered in toffee goo.

"Oh my fucking God, Mae! What are you doing?" Was Abby's tone appreciative? Envious?

Mae no longer cared. Abby could keep her dumpy body and her stupid friends. Mae was on her way to a special gloppy tea party. Imperfects were not invited. Neither was Sandy Bradford. And Mama could rot in hell. Mae slowly lowered her glorious body into the lukewarm caramel slop and declared: "Good stuff in here, Gustav, but it needs perfecting."

And if there was one thing Mae knew how to do insanely well, it was how to be perfect.

The Honeymoon Suite

Jitters

I watch my daughter examine herself in the Honeymoon Suite mirror. She looks foolish—not that I would ever let her know—with that fake lilac headband and fluffy veil, her bosom spilling out over the top of her gown like two mounds of vanilla ice cream. Adele's a big gal, takes after my Swedish Nebraskan family, though I myself have always been a string bean. Luckily her curves are proportional. Plus she inherited Kurt's good looks, his wavy blonde hair, straight nose and killer smile. Adele was spared my horsey plainness, though I'd like to think she inherited a bit of my good sense.

"This is a mistake," Adele moans, then pouts. The red lipstick gives her a demented kewpie doll look. I'm not sure what mistake she's referring to, the veil, the dress, or the whole wedding. I keep quiet.

Adele puts her hands on her waist and squeezes. I can see the strain in her arm muscles. She can barely breathe.

"Stop that, Sweetie," I say. "You look beautiful."

[207]

I walk unsteadily in my high heels to the king-sized hotel bed and sit to take a load off. It's a bed for giants. Rich football stars. All I've ever had is a queen-size. Plenty big now that Kurt drinks himself to sleep in the den most nights, TV blaring. I find him spread eagle and disheveled on the couch come morning.

Kurt and I went to Puerto Vallarta for our honeymoon. He was up for anything. I loved that about him back then. I happily deferred while he struck up conversations with strangers. We spent an entire day with one couple named Carlos and Lupe. Lupe had a pet parrot she found more interesting than humans, especially me. She'd kiss that noisy squawker, lips to beak, which seemed highly unsanitary to me. They spoke Spanish to each other, none of which I understood. The words sounded obscene, especially the bird's.

There was lots of tequila that day, something I was not used to. I'd worn my favorite red vest with the black trim, but because of the drinking and the heat I took it off. I forgot it in the back of a taxi, a spit-and-glue clown car that would never pass inspection here in the States.

Carlos passed out after lunch. Kurt and Lupe danced off together after supper. Kurt came back to our hotel room after midnight, sheepish and apologetic. Lying the first of many lies. Or the first I caught.

"Josh is good for you," I say to Adele as I lay back on the bed and stare up at the mirrored ceiling. Honeymoon Suite, here they come. "He's dependable."

"As. In. Boring." She's squeezing her waist again.

"That's not what I mean," I say. But maybe it is what I mean. Kurt was far from boring and look where that got me. I wonder how things go for Adele and Josh in the sack. But this is not the kind of subject I discuss with my daughter. Or anyone, really. "Let's just say Josh is not going to throw you under any buses."

Adele turns her head from side to side. "Do you think the diamond earrings are overkill?"

"Keep them. They're fantastic," I lie. After many years I've picked up a few tricks.

Joy

Helen's sweaty from her jog along the lake, needs a shower desperately, but that can wait. Meanwhile, the door is reluctant, unobliging. If she knocks, John, wheezing and gray-faced, will trudge across the thickly carpeted floor to let her in. And that won't do. Instead, she dips the swipe card in this way, that way, this again, waiting for the green light. "Fucking excuse for a key," Helen mutters, sure that the maid who's passing by with towel-loaded cart thinks Helen's a lunatic, or worse, an entitled bitch. Finally, the card bids her entry and Helen pushes the ponderous door open.

[209]

John sits in the easy chair, the murder mystery Helen bought him a few weeks prior splayed open on his lap. It makes sense that her husband would choose that god-awful chair. He's spent too many days prone, wasting away in the all-the-bells-and-whistles hospital bed they'd installed in the spare bedroom back home. Helen eyes the cushy, satin-covered king-sized bed in this Honeymoon Suite, and nearly salivates with desire. Oh, to lie down and drift off in a catatonic stupor, she thinks. But no. This weekend is about engagement, so Helen must remain alert.

John hasn't read any of the book. It has been splayed at exactly the same mid-spine spot for days. We're both pretending, she thinks and joins his charade. "Johnny, you'll never guess what I saw on my run," she giggles, believably. "It was hysterical. Totally Chaplin-esque."

She plops on the bed to gaze up at the mirrored ceiling. It's easier to maintain peppiness staring at her own reflection than to look at what remains of her husband.

John exiles the unread book to the side table. "Tell me," he says, his crackled voice a rasp against her heart.

Helen remains light. "There was this woman walking a golden retriever. The dog's pulling her along, and she can barely stay upright, what with a gazillion paper shopping bags knocking against her body."

"Ouch," says John.

"Exactly," Helen agrees. "Then another woman and little girl come ambling up from the opposite direction. The girl is probably around five or six. Definitely a mother and daughter. You know, coloring, body language."

"Like you and Sasha when she was little," John remembers, "Your own mini-me."

Helen studies her reflection, a crumpled, faded version of their daughter, now twenty-eight years old, living in Los Angeles, single, defensive, but gainfully employed. Helen used to worry about her bristly daughter all the time, but John takes up all the anxiety parking spots now.

"Even more mini-me-ish than Sash and me," Helen says. "They were in matching outfits. Awful chartreuse fleece hoodies and striped leggings. Ugg boots."

"Ugh is right," John whispers.

He's punning, thinks Helen. That's good. We're on a roll.

Then John coughs. A wet, gurgly sound. An incessant, internal seepage that usually undoes Helen. But today, she's determined to keep her cool.

"Hold on, hold on," Helen dashes to grab him tissues. The bathroom is enormous. Obscene. There are two sinks, a heart-shaped Jacuzzi tub, lotions and potions for all body parts in a red rattan basket near the bidet. Helen resists the urge to fill the tub, strip off her rancid workout gear and plunge in, jets pummeling her flesh at full blast. Later maybe, she hopes. There are ribbed condoms with hotel insignia embossed on rose-colored foil, nestled like candies in their own special basket next to the tissue box. By booking the Honeymoon Suite, she'd wanted to give the weekend a romantic patina. But if John happened upon these? Overkill, she thinks. Cruel. She shoves the condom basket under the sink, behind a strawberry scented candle that assaults her with saccharine fumes as she shuts the cabinet door.

John is lying on the bed when she returns. He's staring at his reflection, his face a grimacing ashen mask. He's a bag of loose, wobbly objects jumbled inside sweatpants and sweatshirt. Shriveled here, bloated there.

Helen places the tissue box gingerly in the concave dip that used to be John's flabby stomach. Who needs a TV tray? John joked, just last week, as he snacked on pretzels from the same spot.

Helen lies down beside him. "Where was I?" She grabs his ice-cold hand.

"How the hell would I know?" John's testy. He blames the medication, but really, he hasn't had patience for her stories in years. "Something about a kid and her mother in ugly clothes. Before that, something about a big dog and grocery bags."

Why do I even try? Helen wants to say. Even when dying, you're a nasty son of a bitch. But she's a bulldozer and continues with extra verve. "So, the mom is also loaded with grocery bags, and her kid has an ice cream cone. The kid sees the dog and jumps for joy. She starts running towards the dog and the dog starts tugging on its leash to get to her."

"Sounds like a shit show," says John, "When does it get funny?"

Helen squeezes his hand hard. She wants to crush it, feel his bones splinter. She has impulses like this quite often, ones she would never, or at least hasn't, acted upon. She imagines shards turning to chalk within the sack of his skin. Along with these impulses, Helen also has Let's get on with this death thing already thoughts. But more often, she has When you go, the hole in my life will be so enormous I just might have to jump in it and disappear myself thoughts. I love you thoughts.

Helen sighs. "Come on. Let me finish."

John closes his eyes and nods, feebly.

"The dog owner loses her grip on the leash and the dog skitters towards the kid," Helen's so chipper, it's like she's channeled an entire cheerleading squad. "Both women run behind their separate charges with bags swinging away. Then the bags start ripping. Produce goes flying, granola hits the pavement, eggs go splat, tomatoes explode, milk streams everywhere." She pauses for effect.

"That's it?" John coughs again.

You usually love slapstick, Helen thinks, releasing her husband's hand. This tidbit has all the right elements of mayhem and buffoonery, of near disaster belonging to someone else. "No, there's more. The dog reaches the little girl and nips the ice cream cone out of her hand and devours the entire thing," Helen's talking so fast she sounds like a speed freak. "The silly beast's snout is covered in chocolate. By the time the women get there, the dog is slobbering chocolate kisses all over the kid's face, the two of them as happy as can be. The End."

John wheezes, but says nothing.

You're supposed to be laughing, you old grump, Helen thinks. "Most kids would've been reduced to tears." She can see his deflated chest rise and fall next to her out of the corner of her eye. "Sash would've been whiny for the rest of the day at that age."

"It's bad for dogs," John opens his eyes and takes a tissue to wipe phlegmy residue from the corners of his cracked lips.

"What the fuck, Johnny," Helen pounds the satin bedspread in frustration. "How can a child's love be bad for a dog?"

John lies still as stone, maybe practicing for the inevitable. "Not love. Chocolate. It's toxic. If dogs eat too much of it they can die."

The air is molten, but John can't tolerate air conditioning anymore, and the Honeymoon Suite windows don't open. The mirrored ceiling doppelgangers stare down at Helen and John and they stare back. Everyone gasps for breath.

Her Giant Sequoia

If only Ryan could stop crying, but the damn tears keep coming, gushing like geysers, dribbling down hot cheeks, flooding the creases of his quivering jowls. Ryan hasn't bawled like this since he was a kid. He's heaving relentless sobs that feel lethal, like an asthmatic gasping for breath. But Ryan's not ill, he's just pathetic. He's already soaked the pocket square he'd folded—just in case—in the inner pocket of his tuxedo. His store-bought tuxedo. Now he clutches that damp and useless rag in a trembling hand. He's too stunned to get off his ass and grab tissues from the obscenely huge strawberry-stenched bathroom of this Honeymoon Suite. Ryan had been prepared to cry on this momentous day, his wedding day, the day he and Julie were to bind themselves like twisted ribbons. Knotted at both ends. Together forever. But Ryan had anticipated tears of joy, of ecstatic release, not these clucking wails.

Ryan sinks to the floor, his cummerbund a vise grip as he doubles over sturdy haunches.

"Tree trunks," Julie had sighed, stroking his linebacker thighs a mere two nights before, "My very own giant sequoia."

Julie and her airy fairy homilies. What did Ryan expect, falling in love with a girl raised by hippies on a commune outside Bolinas? Nothing Julie ever said made much sense. What made sense was how she held Ryan captive with those sighs, the sex, her model looks. Her boobs, for God's sake, what a pair. What he'd thought made sense was Julie choosing Ryan over all those other dudes. That banker Chet, the one who scurried around San Fran on a dorky recumbent bike. Elliot, the egghead from Harvard who did some-kind-of-something that was pure gobbletygook to Ryan. When Julie explained it, Ryan nodded and aha'd, pretending to comprehend.

But Ryan was her giant sequoia. Her big, dumb, football-playing idiot with a pro ball contract. A millionaire by way of grunting, passing, sweating, running, colliding, assaulting. Her big lug who offered rescuing hands to tackled compadres and opponents alike. Genuinely nice, the kind of guy who glugged Gatorade from a spigot attached to a plastic tub, but always made sure to leave enough swigs for the next thirsty beast.

Julie's text came in before the wedding guests scurried out of the church like a bunch of released convicts. For over an hour they'd had to sit in the pews, fidgeting as they watched Ryan stare down the aisle, wiping droplet after droplet of sweat from his shelf-like brow. All of them waiting for Julie to be escorted by Willow and Raven, her dickweed parents with little or no brain cells left after all the pot they'd grown, smoked, sold. Who could blame anyone for wanting to flee the church once Ryan looked up from his buzzing phone and said in a flailing, choked voice that careened across two octaves:

"The wedding is off, folks. You can all go on home."

In the end Egghead Elliot scored the touchdown. Now Ryan sits in this Honeymoon Suite alone, leaning massive shoulders against the satin spread of a bed made for the likes of him. A king-sized atrocity, a squishy, bouncy crash pad for fucking, for fermenting in newlywed juices. Instead this jilted giant is deep in his own cavernous stew.

Maid Service

Snooping through opened luggage, lingerie on the floor, or the goopy residue on room service trays tells me only so much. I know the whole story after the lovers have gone for good, when all that's left are their scents, invisible fumes, whiffs of the essential. More often than not, the air in here is ripe with desire. But sometimes the place is filled with a mournful stench. I've gotten more than one nose full of despair.

The minute I pushed my cart through the door just now, I could tell that last couple had quite a racy time. Her scent mixed with his. Like my abuela's backyard: cilantro and wet mutt. Kind of nasty, right? But it's a loving stink.

[217]

Which smell is hers and which is his? Your guess is as good as mine. Fumes all over the place from those two, even behind that ugly upright chair. Their smells are never separate, which tells me what I need to know.

They don't know how lucky they are. Or maybe they do.

When Carlos was an infant, I had to bring him to work a bunch of times. It was right after Freddy left me. Left us. I figured out a way to hide Carlos from that bitch supervisor, Roberta. I wedged his little body between stacks of towels, rolled my cart down the halls like I was pushing a pyramid of crystal goblets, each nubby carpet bump a possible disaster. Carlos slept most of the time back then, which was lucky. Thank God he stayed quiet. When I got in each room, I'd take him out and lay him in the center of the bed. This king-sized was the best, even if he woke up. I'd plop him in the center and watch him wiggle his little brown arms and legs, like an upside down beetle. So happy. Laughing like a crazy drunken fool staring up at his reflection in that porno ceiling. This bed is so huge I didn't have to worry about him sliding off the edge. I could clean the whole place without that freaked out lump in my throat, my heart beating like a tom-tom drum, which was how it was in all the regular rooms.

Maybe that's why I'm so good at reading the vibe in here. Maybe I'm psychic. I have good associations with this humongous Honeymoon Suite, with its big-ass bed, giant vat of a bathtub, and embarrassing mirrored ceiling.

So, you want to know more about that last couple? I give them two years tops. A baby will come. They'll each love that baby with such smelly sweetness. They'll make two new perfumes, each a blend with that baby. But this odor? This soppy dog and cilantro scent? This sexy funk? Breathe deep, my friend. This may be the last of it, right here.

Tossed

The bell rang twenty minutes earlier than expected. I took one last look around the studio, then raced through the apartment towards the door. I hadn't brushed my teeth yet. My mouth was coated in a fermenting residue of coffee and bacon. At least it's grass-fed bacon from the farmer's market, I told myself, as if the provenance of my breakfast would make any difference to how my breath might stink.

I opened the door, inhaling as I said, "Hi Anita! So great to see you again."

It had been almost fifteen years since I'd seen Anita Mego in person. Still tiny, height-wise, she was now round and squat, cloaked in a red cape with beaded fringe, her forehead in line with my boobs. Anita's hair, formerly brown and Brillo-pad-ish, was platinum blonde and cut in a stick-straight bob. Red-tinted glasses perched on her chubby cheeks like the headlights on a Toon Town car. No, it wasn't great to see her again. It was disturbing.

She squinted at me. "How do we know each other again?"

"Um, I think Donald told you about me."

"Oh yeah," she smiled. "Donald. I love Donald. Don't you just love Donald?"

Donald, my well-connected culturati second cousin, was successful enough to be friends with Anita, and nice enough to call in a favor for less successful me. Anita was an art star in a sub-section of the New York Art World I aspired to be part of. She was the big cheese planted in the center of the platter. I'd been sitting at the edge of the platter for over ten years, a stale cracker no one wanted to eat. Inclusion in a few group shows at crummy galleries and not-for-profit spaces, a handful of sales to friends of my parents, one mention on an obscure culture website, and one review written by my former college roommate. This was my pathetic resume of meager success.

Pathologically shy as a child, and still socially inept, I'd been to my fair share of art openings and tried my best to schmooze. But all I'd end up with were countless headaches after too many truncated conversations and plastic cups of cheap white wine. The artists I knew personally who had made it big had done so by overcoming their insecurities and basic insanity by constantly networking with awe-inspiring relentlessness. But Anita Mego seemed different. At least to me, she was the real deal. I thought her work was pure and unpretentious. She was an artist's artist, rarely seen at openings or pounding the Chelsea pavements on a Saturday afternoon. So while I didn't exactly love cousin

Donald, I liked him well enough, more so now that he'd recommended me to Anita who was known to foster the careers of younger female sculptors. Women she considered her creative offspring. God how I longed to be adopted.

"Sure. I, ah, love Donald," I said. "But actually you and I met fifteen years ago. At RISD." Please remember, I thought. I was an eager, starry-eyed twenty-one-year-old artiste, and you were a thirty-something sprite, ninety pounds of white heat with a punk hairdo. You were inspiring, urgent, insistent. You spoke about 'the feminist imperative to reclaim the three dimensions'. You told me my work was 'cool.'

"RISD?" Anita squinted again. "It's a bitch to keep track of all those school visits. What the hell did I do there?"

"You gave a lecture on your work. Afterwards you did crits on senior thesis projects." She had stood in front of my cubicle squinting—not unlike the way she was squinting now—at my 'body' of work; semi-realistic, but lopsided and lazy figures in groups of three to five. Each 'family' had one shared attribute; purple wormlike arms, lopsided breasts, no ears. One group was blessed with cloven hooves. It was pretentious, as student work usually is, and arguably, should be. If nothing else, my blobby sculptures did a good job hiding my weakness at proportional rendering.

How well I remembered when Anita said, "Now this. Yeah this. This is some cool stuff," before she pranced over to Adam Schechtner's adjacent cubicle, where she grunted hostilely at his Judd-ian cubes and said nothing. At 7 p.m. she was ushered away by the head of the department for a dinner with selected faculty. As the double metal doors closed behind her and her academic entourage, Adam snarked, "She's full of shit. She's not even that great an artist."

I nodded in agreement. But secretly I prayed Anita was a seer and a saint.

Now, fifteen years later, Anita Mego stood in my grown-up vestibule peering at me as if I were an indecipherable set of directions to a place she didn't want to go to. "I'm sorry, Doll," she shrugged. "No recuerdo. You'll have to bear with me. This menopause stuff is for the birds. I can't even remember if I took a dump this morning or not."

"That's okay," I shrugged. "I mean, that you don't remember me. Not that you're going through menopause. That sucks."

"Just you wait." She examined me over the rim of her glasses, tipping her chin down, her double chin bulging like a bullfrog's. "Before you know it, hot flashes, crankiness, dementia, insomnia."

"Wow."

"No libido. Dry everything, actually. Hair, skin, the works."

"Oh, really," I nodded sympathetically.

"Totally answers the 'B' question. You have any?"

"Any what?" I asked.

"Babies."

It would've been an innocuous question, if asked by someone else. But from childless, successful Anita Mego to younger, wannabe me, it was a loaded inquiry. Motherhood was viewed by many artists of her generation as the kiss of death to any 'serious' career. Not that my own generation was any clearer on the issue. At thirty-six, I was still clinging to my last few biological clock years, swimming in a gobbletygook of confusion, ambition, creative drive, and inertia.

"No," I finally answered.

"Oh," she lightened up.

"Not yet."

"Oh," she darkened.

"We haven't really decided if we want to. My husband and I, that is."

That was a lie. Milo had wanted to start a family for years, having happily shed his artistic mantle immediately after graduation. "Enough of that," he said as we rattled our way south on I-95 in our crappy Toyota truck, away from art school and bound for the first in a series of roach-infested far, far East Village walk ups. "You can carry the torch for both of us." Milo wasn't simple, but he had simple needs. He was the lucky one, free from the burden of creative aspirations, happy with his well-paying job as head systems administrator for a hot shit everybody-wanted-to-work-there web-based corporation. I was the unlucky complicator, dragging my ambivalent parenting heels, waiting for a sign from the procreation gods.

Anita snorted. "It's your life."

Was it? I wondered. "So, um, please come in."

"I hope it's okay that I brought my baby girl," she said, beaming suddenly.

Holy shit. I had totally misread her. She wasn't anti-baby. She had a baby. A baby! What did this mean? Should I have answered the 'B' question differently? But where was the baby? Maybe she had it hidden under the folds of her poncho.

"Of course it's okay," I said. "Where is she? I can't wait to meet her."

Anita turned back towards the hallway and called, "Scarlett, come, come girl...thaaat's it, come to Mama."

A tiny ratlike dog skittered from around the corner, where it had been doing God-knows-what in front of my neighbor's door.

"Oh. A dog," I said.

Anita grunted as she stooped to scoop Scarlett up, then stood triumphantly, holding the mongrel under her arm like a football. "Is that a problem?"

I thought of my sculptures, fragile little beasts themselves, covering my studio floor.

"No," I smiled. "Not a problem. Come on in."

Anita pushed past me into the living room, scrutinizing my belongings as if she were an estate assessor. She picked up a vase, brushed her hand across a lamp shade. She stared up at the chandelier I'd inherited from my grandmother. She examined the collection of tiny clay pots lining the mantle, then repositioned them in a different configuration. She might as well have plucked out my fingernails.

"Is that a Daniel Wiener?" she finally spoke, pointing with her free hand to a carved colorful wall piece, that was, in fact a Daniel Wiener.

"Yes," I said proudly. "My husband bought it for me for my 35th birthday last year. I'm a big fan."

She shrugged. "Daniel's always good. But I liked his earlier work better."

Scarlett started wiggling and barking.

"Do you mind if I put her down?" Anita asked.

"I guess, but—"

Anita didn't wait for my response. She plopped Scarlett down on the shag rug, professionally cleaned two days earlier for the first time in ten years. Scarlett went gaga, rolling around as if the wool fibers were covered in dog pheromones. She twisted and rubbed her bristly little back, spread eagle and panting. Next she flipped over and burrowed her snout so deep in the pile all that remained visible were two pointy, devilish ears.

"She really digs your rug," Anita giggled.

All I could think of was doggie dandruff and drool.

"Could be because I don't have any rugs in my loft," Anita gazed around at my tchocke-filled home. "Actually. I don't have much of anything. I'm a minimalist when it comes to home decor. I find it gets in the way of my creative drive."

I forced a smile. "Shall we go into the studio?"

Anita shrugged. "I'm easy."

I looked down at Scarlett, who'd resumed back-humping. "Would you mind holding Scarlett while we're in there? My work is all over the floor."

"If you really need me to," Anita half-groaned.

"Great! Thanks!" I chirped, hyper-cheerleader, hoping to turn this game around.

Anita crouched again. "Come on Scarala. Come to Mama." Scarlett scurried towards her executing an impressive doggie leap into waiting arms. "That's my girl. My wooshy, mooshy girl." Anita closed her eyes and let Scarlett go to town, licking her fleshy cheeks, chin, nose, her rubbery neck.

Blech, I thought as I walked towards my studio. Blech, blech, blech. I had to wait by the studio door for a few awkward minutes while Anita finished her lovefest and finally rose from the floor.

+++++++

Earlier that morning, hours before the premature arrival of Anita Mego, while the coffeemaker gurgled and Milo listened to the radio, I headed towards my studio, the spare room at the rear of our apartment. I opened the door slowly, pretending I was about to see my work for the first time. This was one of my pre-studio visit rituals, a mind game that rarely ended well. I don't know why I kept up with this stupid charade. It was masochistic. Whenever I tried to look at my work with 'fresh' eyes, I felt a wash of disappointment.

The door swung open and I gazed at my sculptures. I made tiny figures; each one could fit in the palm of a hand. They were delicate little beings, constructed of glass, feathers, and thin wire. There were hundreds of them arranged like a battalion of toy soldiers on my studio floor.

During her lecture at RISD, Anita had said, "Art that is diminutive in scale can have the resonance and power of a nuclear bomb." It became my mantra. I tore out the page I'd written it on and tacked it to every studio wall I'd had in the intervening years. I planned to show it to her later that day. She would be blown away by my loyalty to the cause, fifteen years hence.

"They're your embryos," Milo exclaimed. He'd abandoned Morning Edition to join me, slurping his coffee as he looked over my shoulder and down at the floor. "Ours, maybe."

"Well?" I said.

"Well what?"

"Do you think Anita will like my work?"

[229]

"Gimme a break," he groaned and started back towards the kitchen.

"Wait!"

"Wait for what?" Milo stopped, but didn't turn around. "Are you ever going to be ready?"

"Ready for Anita?" I could see the hints of a bald spot. Pink scalp skin, newly naked at the back of Milo's skull.

His shoulders sagged. "I couldn't give a flying fuck about Anita Mego." Milo finally faced me, looking tired even though I knew he'd just gotten a solid eight hours of sleep. "I'm talking about babies, Stella. Not art."

"Oh."

"Your little sculpture dudes are brilliant," he smiled weakly. "Just holler when you want to make a flesh and blood one."

I was about to say, sure, I'll holler. Soon. Maybe. But Milo had already turned, leaving me knotted, ready to start his straightforward day.

+++++++

Anita stood in one spot, looked down at my precious battalion and said absolutely nothing. Not a word, good, bad, or indifferent about my sculptures, or anything else, until Scarlett started to squirm in her arms.

"I'm sorry," she said to Scarlett. What I got, without apology, was, "I could put her out in the apartment while we're in here."

Wow, I thought. Anita wants to stay in my studio alone. "Sure," I said, back in cheerleader mode. My rug would pay the price, but I was willing to let Scarlett run amok with her odd little doggie urges, while I hopefully got something—anything—from Anita.

Anita put Scarlett down next to one of my favorite figures. The dog sniffed it and knocked it over.

"No, no Scarlett," Anita said calmly. "We don't play with the art. You know better than that."

Better than what? I wanted to yell. She's just a fucking dog doing what dogs do naturally: sniffing, rubbing, licking. Wreaking havoc.

Anita herded Scarlett towards the door. "Now scoot. Go on. Play out there. Mommy will be done soon."

Scarlett raced through the apartment, tiny claws click-clicking like castanets on the wood floor.

Anita smiled at me. "Don't worry. She'll be fine."

"She's adorable," I lied. She knows exactly where she's going, I thought. Creepy little alien beast.

"She is, isn't she? Oy. I need to plotz." Anita walked to the far end of the studio and collapsed in to my studio chair. She pulled out her iPhone and held it face up in her hand. "I may be getting an important call from Germany. My dealer over there is giving me major agita. Wants me to accept a huge discount on a sale to some Baron Somebody-Somebody. Don't you hate it when dealers start to pull rank?"

I'd never had a dealer, of any nationality. I was a free agent, better known as a nobody. I had nothing to say. I was all out of pep rally enthusiasm, which didn't matter because Anita did all the talking. She leaned back in the chair letting off hot air like a slowly deflating Macy's Thanksgiving Day balloon. She bitched about the German. She moaned about her lagging overseas sales. She criticized a well-respected female artist of her generation. She trashed a contemporary of mine.

For half an hour she went on and on with no mention of my work, no acknowledgment of the tiny labors of love strewn at her feet. All I got was her wide ass-plotzing on my favorite chair—ironically, a chair I'd had in my cubicle studio at RISD at our only other encounter, the encounter Anita had totally forgotten. It was an authentic Saarinen Womb chair I'd bought my sophomore year. A wealthy Brown student was going abroad, thus hastily divesting of all her worldly goods, and so the chair became mine for a song. I'd accumulated other cool stuff over the years, but none of it was ever as good, or worldly, as my beloved chair. Which Anita abruptly rose from when she was done venting, pontificating, and blatantly bragging.

"Jesus," she said, looking at the old fashioned alarm clock I kept on a shelf. "Is it really eleven already? I've gotta split. Scarlett's going to the vet. She needs her shots for China. Did I tell you about the retrospective I'm having in Shanghai?"

"No," I sighed. "You didn't mention that one."

Anita almost stepped on one of my pieces as she left the studio. I told myself that if she had, I would've raised bloody hell, and not continued in woozy suck-up mode. But she didn't step on one. And to be honest, I probably would've sucked it up anyhow. My desperate art outsider nose was still that ridiculously brown, even after this lame excuse for a studio visit.

"Scarlett," she called as we approached the living room. "Come to Mama!"

Scarlett poked her head up from behind a sofa cushion. I noticed tufts of white batting attached to her whiskers. We locked looks, Scarlett's gaze all guilty teenage shoplifter. You fucking rodent, I screamed inside. You've eaten my couch.

Scarlett broke eye contact and bee-lined for Mama. They had another slobbery lovefest, fifth-wheeling me to the ozone. I felt like pelting them both with the sea glass I kept in a bowl on my coffee table.

Finally, the licking and panting ended. "I gotta pee like a racehorse," said Anita. "Another menopause affliction. The whole inner apparatus down there shifts in some cockamimie way and puts pressure on your bladder. I'm up at least three times a night. And don't get me started on what happens if I drink more than one cup of coffee. Where's your bathroom?"

"It's in there." I hiked an unenthusiastic thumb.

Anita thrust Scarlett in my direction. "She has this thing about flushing toilets. They scare her to death, poor little sweetie."

Scarlett snarled. I could see bits of couch thread stuck between her tiny shark-like teeth.

Anita chuckled. "Maybe I'll just put her on the floor again."

"Good idea." I said through clenched teeth.

Scarlett ran back to the rug as soon as the bathroom door shut. I walked up behind her. She was deep in to nose-burrowing, a goddamn shag addict unaware that I towered over her, eyeing her tiny rump. I inched closer. Scarlett snuffled obliviously, obsessively, undeterred.

I waited until I heard the toilet flush and the sink water run. It was something between a kick and a lift. Scarlett flew through the air, like a punted hacky sack. She yelped mid-flight, then landed on her belly with a dull thud. Motionless, her eyes blank, her little doggie legs splayed unnaturally wide like a miniature bear rug.

Honestly? My first thought was; there goes any chance you ever had of being one of Anita's chosen few. Instead you'll be the sculptor who killed her Chihuahua. That will be your one and only art world claim to fame.

But wouldn't you know it, just I began feeling overwhelmed with guilt and remorse, Scarlett righted herself. No broken doggie bones, no obvious signs of injury. She stared at me, shivering like she was on an ice floe in Antarctica.

I bared my teeth and growled. Scarlett scrambled under the couch whimpering until Anita returned.

It was a pathetic victory, but one I held firmly as I ushered them out the door and watched as they kerplumbled down the steep steps of my building's stoop, Scarlett trailing behind Anita at the umbilical end of a lime green leash.

Afterwards, I went back into the studio and sat in my chair, reclaiming my throne. My Anita quote was still tacked to the wall by my window on yellowing paper. Meanwhile, my tiny army stood at attention, awaiting orders. I felt restless, ready to fight, but it wasn't this battle.

I stood to leave. "Don't worry guys," I said, "I'll be back. Sometime."

Then I called Milo.

"I'm hollering," I whispered into the phone. "I'm ready. Can you hear me?"

Acknowledgements

My most heartfelt thanks to:

The editors and publishers who loved these tales and gave them first homes in phenomenal publications.

My generous friends and colleagues who took the time to read one or more of these stories, especially those who've sung my praises when I'm sure they had much better things to do.

Candy Adriance, Susan Bruce, Hope Davis, and Ann Glickman for their friendship, editorial prowess, inspiration and support.

Jan Clausen, Tessa Hadley and Stephen Allen Gurganus who took me seriously, and whose words of wisdom made a world of difference.

Leanna Gruhn for her savvy edits, layout and marketing skills.

Alison Seiffer for her artistic genius and visual understanding of the word "subversive."

My agent Zoe Sandler for her belief in me and what I write.

Jerry Brennan of Tortoise Books for snatching up this collection and being as responsive and smart an editor-publisher as I could ever hope for.

My creative, and beautiful sisters Naomi, Ilya and Hannah for reading with intelligence and humor.

My astounding mother Selma for her enthusiasm towards all my creative pursuits and always sharing her passion for books.

Noa Isabella Kaltman Wiener for being the reason for everything.

Daniel Wiener for loving me and for caring as much about this book as I do, if not more.

The following stories first appeared in:

"Snow Day!" and "Tossed" in *Across The Margin*
"Tossed" and "Boss Man," with music and art, in *Storychord*
"A Melody" in *The 34th Parallel Magazine*
"Bigfoot" in *The Stockholm Review of Literature*
"Freedom" in *Luna Luna Magazine*
"Staggerwing" in *Atticus Review*
"Stay A While" and "Blossoms" in *Joyland Magazine*
"Jitters" (from "The Honeymoon Suite") in *The Victoria Rose*
"Her Giant Sequoia" (from "The Honeymoon Suite") in *Chicago Literati*
"Maid Service" (from "The Honeymoon Suite") in *Whiskey Paper*
"The Honeymoon Suite" in Tortoise Books' *Saudade: The Pleasure You Suffer*

About the Author

Alice Kaltman is a writer and surfer who splits her time between Brooklyn and Montauk, New York. Her short fiction appears in numerous journals including *Joyland*, *Whiskey Paper*, *Storychord*, *The Stockholm Review*, *Atticus Review*, and *Chicago Literati*, and in print anthologies including Tortoise Books' *Saudade: The Pleasure You Suffer*. Her website is pretty: www.alicekaltman.com

Made in the USA
Middletown, DE
20 September 2016